HURRICANE OF MAGIC

THE VOODOO DOLLS BOOK TWO

J.L. HENDRICKS

First Edition June, 2017

All rights reserved. Copyright © 2017 J.L. Hendricks

Editor: Rebecca Reddell

Illustrator: Rebecca Frank

❀ Created with Vellum

1

JENNA

"*O*omph!" I landed on my butt - hard! This fighting wasn't getting any easier. In fact, it was getting tougher.

"Dude, you better not mess up my pants! They're brand new." I hated it when vampires attacked for no good reason.

"Doll, I wouldn't worry about your pants if I were you." The vampire who threw me to the ground was coming back to get me again, but I was ready this time.

With a roundhouse kick Rico taught me, I got the guy in the gut. His eyes narrowed, and he actually seemed shocked I was able to get in a good kick. These past six months have done wonders for my fighting ability. Well, to be honest, it was non-existent before Rico and his pack took me and my sisters under their wing.

The vamp backed up a few steps to get out of the reach of my legs. Next thing I knew, the blood-sucker was behind me and had his arm around my neck. Grabbing his arm, I bent at my waist and tossed him over my shoulder. Again, he seemed stunned I was fighting back.

"Grrr, I'm done playing with you. You are going to submit to me - tonight!" He licked his lips and focused on the throbbing vein in my neck.

I'll be honest; it was tiring fighting him. My skills were improving daily, but fighting an actual vampire, when I knew my life was on the line, was very different from sparring with the wolf-shifters who happened to be my friends.

It was time for the big guns.

Pulling out the wooden stake from inside my jacket, I got into my fighting stance. Feet spread shoulder width apart, knees bent, and fists out in front of my chest. One hand gripped the stake and was ready to strike the second this blood-sucker was close enough.

"Okay, Buffy. You got me. I surrender." The vampire was very sarcastic. He must have been a newer vamp if he knew that pop-culture reference.

"Funny, I don't take you for the Spike kinda guy. You seem like the kinda guy who gets spiked." I smirked.

"If I remember correctly, Spike and Buffy got it on more times than anyone can count. I'm up for the same relationship, if you think you can handle me." His smile disgusted me.

This guy was nothing like Spike. Real vampires weren't like what we watched on TV either. They were more evil and more interested in having humans be their daily blood supply than friends.

"Not in this life creep." I moved closer to him. The sooner I killed him, the better. He gave me the creeps.

His wicked smile was enough to gag on. "Hmm, sounds like you're ready for the next life. Good. Let's get this going. I'm hungry, and your blood is calling to me."

"Shut up and make your move, fangboy. I'm ready to get

home and take a nice, long, hot bath. Your stink is all over me." I blinked, and he was next to me.

Spinning around, I slammed the steak into his chest but missed his heart. Grunting I said, "This is harder than Buffy made it look."

The vampire laughed and pulled the stake out of his chest. Throwing it far away, he moved behind me. Grabbing my hair, he pulled back my head to give him access to my neck. I could hear him smack his lips before he bit down.

"Ahhh!" I screamed when his fangs broke the skin. As the pain made its way through my head, I realized I needed to do something and fast.

"You're right. I do want to jump your bones. The bad guys are always the best lovers. Let go of me, and I'll be happy to go with you." It was the only thing I could think of to get his fangs off my neck.

He was way too strong for me to pull away from. If I didn't stop him, I'd be too weak to fight him when he did let go.

He pulled his head back and licked my blood off his lips, like it was ice cream. "Hmmm, your blood is sweeter than it smells. I can't wait to get you back to my room. You made the right choice." He licked my neck and lightly nibbled on my ear.

It sent chills of disgust up and down my spine. How could anyone enjoy this? It hurt!

"What's your name?" I wanted to be able to tell Rico who I killed tonight, if I made it out of here alive.

"You can call me, Spike, if you like." He continued to kiss my neck and ear. If he didn't let me go soon, I'd be puking.

"No, your real name. What do I call you in front of others?" If I kept him talking, maybe he would begin to relax and let go of me, or give me a chance to grab the other stake in my boot.

"Master. All acolytes call me master. However, when we are alone, you may address me as Derek." He turned me around and kissed my mouth full on. GROSS!

His tongue tried to part my lips. I could taste my own coppery blood as he tried to get me to open my mouth for his tongue. This was it. How far do I let him go before I fight back?

I couldn't do it.

Pushing him back I reached down with one arm for the stake in my boot and pulled it out while he was laughing.

"I knew you were lying, little hunter. Good, this just makes it all the sweeter." He lunged at me.

This time I did hit the mark.

With wide eyes, he looked down at his chest before he slumped to the ground.

I wish it was like in the movies or TV shows. Stake a vamp and poof. But no. In real life their lifeless body is still there.

Joseph, the pack's Alchemist, told us that the vamp's bodies have to be set out where the sunlight will hit them in the morning. Then the bodies go poof. However, the body needs to be put in a place where no one will get to it before the sun comes up. If regular humans found it, they would know vampires were real.

I wished I could just dump it in a trash bin, but then the sun wouldn't hit it. Hiding it in bushes wouldn't work either, not enough rays from the sun would get to it. Besides, animals would probably find it before enough sunlight did hit the body.

Leaving it out in the open was certainly not an option.

Pulling my phone from my jacket pocket I dialed Rico.

Not long after I met Rico, we hired him to help us find a friend of ours who had been abducted by a vampire. The cops were no help to Acadia's sisters when they reported her missing. Rico went down to the police station, and they gave him the CCTV footage showing Acadia leaving a nightclub with a vampire.

Rico and his pack protected New Orleans and her inhabitants. He was also the CEO of a very successful private investigation firm. Sometimes, he even worked with the local police. They respected him so much, they gave him whatever he asked for.

"Hey, Jenna! What's up?" Rico answered on the second ring.

"Hi, Rico. I could use some help." Sighing, I told him what happened.

"YOU WHAT? Of all people, I would think you would know better than to go out at night all alone. What were you thinking?" I could hear his anger, as I'm sure anyone within several blocks of him could.

I pulled the phone away from my ear and shook my head. That guy had a set of lungs on him.

"I thought it would be safe to go out for Chinese. There's this little hole in the wall only a few blocks from my apartment. It was never an issue before. I'm actually surprised no one came running when I screamed." This was not going well.

"Where exactly are you? I'll see who's the closest and send them to you. Is there a store or restaurant you can wait inside of?"

"Um, I'm in an alley close to the Chinese restaurant, Uncle Wong's. I'll head there. What do I do about the body?" I looked around at my surroundings and noticed a few things I could use to cover up the body temporarily.

"Never mind, I'll just put some trash over him. I doubt anyone will look too closely at stinking garbage." Walking over to the dumpster I eyed earlier, I picked up some mostly empty boxes and dumped the contents on the vamp.

Great, it was rotting vegetables. At least the stench would keep away any lookie-loos.

2

JENNA

I heaved a huge sigh of relief when I walked into Uncle Wong's. "Hey, Jimmie. Do you have my order ready?"

"Jenna? What happened to you? Why do you have blood on your neck and shirt?" Jimmie was actually Uncle Wong.

Who ever heard of a Chinese restaurant called Uncle Jimmie's? Wong isn't even his last name, it's Ang. Not the best name for a restaurant. I liked the name Uncle Wong, it flowed off the tongue.

"I was attacked in the alley." I held up my hands when Jimmie started to get upset.

"I called a friend, and he's sending someone to help me. I'll be ok after I get some of your famous wonton soup and a bath." Sitting down in a chair, I looked to the TV he had in the bar area. It was currently showing the weather report.

Jimmie rushed into the back and came out within a minute carrying a steaming hot cup of wonton soup. "Here, take this while you wait. It'll help give you nourishment. Can I get you some tea? I think tea would be good." He ran to the back again.

I called out, "Thanks, Jimmie! It looks worse than what it really is."

Looking around, I noticed there weren't any other customers in the place. Normally, Uncle Wong's was really busy this time of night. It was close to eleven at night, but he always had to make people leave when they closed at one in the morning. Wong's was a very popular place to hit up after the clubs or the parades.

Since no one was around, I put the bowl to my lips and slurped it. Jimmie wouldn't care. "Mmm, this is exactly what I needed! Thanks, Jimmie."

He walked out of the kitchen with a cup of piping hot tea. I could see the steam coming off the cup. "Drink this, and don't slurp my wonton soup! It's not ladylike." Jimmie pursed his lips and took the seat next to me.

"Tell me, what happened? Who did this to you? And where are they? Should I get my cousin to teach this animal some manners?" Jimmie's cousin was in a gang.

I wanted nothing to do with them. I had enough trouble just keeping up with a pack of wolf-shifters.

"I don't think you have to worry about him. He won't be coming around here." Did Jimmie know the truth? How should I handle this?

A little voice in my head said *Change the topic.*

"Jimmie, I thought the hurricane was going to dissipate before hitting land? According to the news," I pointed to the TV over the bar. "It looks like we might be seeing another hurricane hit our poor town. Turn up the volume. I want to know when it's going to hit land."

"Don't worry, it won't be hitting until sometime tomorrow early afternoon. Sasha, she's my favorite weather girl, said it wouldn't be any stronger than a cat 2. She thinks it might even be downgraded to a tropical storm by then." Jimmie had goo-goo eyes for Sasha, the local weather girl.

She wore those super low-cut and very tight dresses that the men loved so much. I didn't think much of her, she was usually wrong. However, most of the time all of the weather people were wrong, didn't matter how hot they were.

"Is that why the place is empty? Are people evacuating? Has it been ordered yet?" I looked over my shoulder at all of the empty tables and booths.

"We closed early tonight. I only stayed here for you to pick up your order. When you came in, I was in the middle of packaging all of our leftovers to take on the road. I was going to leave once it was all packed up. Now I know why you were so late." Jimmie scrunched his nose.

"Jenna, you need a bath. Sorry, but you stink." He leaned away from me enough to let me know he wasn't kidding.

"Sorry, Jimmie. I fought back. We were in an alley that was filled with rotten vegetables and who knows what else. Probably dead rats too." I shivered.

We both turned when the bell above the door rang.

"Damien! Thank you so much for coming so quickly! Were you the closest?" I stood up to greet my friend who also happened to be a pretty tough wolf-shifter and the pack's beta.

"Jenna, thank goodness! Rico is out of his mind with worry! Hi, Jimmie! You have any more food? I think you're going to be inundated with a few pack members." Damien came over and was about to hug me, but he scrunched his nose and stepped back.

"Jenna, you need a shower. Badly." He fanned his nose.

"Sure thing, Damien. How many are coming?" Jimmie asked when he stood up.

"Probably at least a dozen. You know how they get when

they're patrolling. I would imagine they're going to be very hungry." Damien took a seat at my table.

When Jimmie went to the back, I leaned forward and whispered, "Does Jimmie know? About you guys?"

"Of course, most of the shop and restaurant owners who stay open really late have had run-ins with vampires. Not all know we're shifters, but Jimmie does. One of my guys saved him and his wife from an attack a few years back. Now, this is one of our favorite places to patrol. Jimmie always gives us wonton soup when we come in." Damien looked up to the TV.

No wonder Jimmie's wife was never here at night.

"Did you see the report? Looks like the city is going to get hit with a hurricane after all. What do you guys do during hurricanes? Do you evac?" I had never considered what they would do during an emergency.

Last hurricane season I didn't know these guys. This was the first one heading our way since I'd met them.

"We have a place a few hours north of here. If the hurricane is projected to be cat 4 or above, we send our young and elderly there for safety. Otherwise, we can withstand quite a bit."

"Yeah, you guys are pretty tough and fast." I reached up and massaged my neck close to where the stupid vamp bit me. The muscles were sore. Stupid vamps!

"How much did he drink from you?" Damien's eyes darkened when he looked at my neck.

"Not a lot. I tricked him into letting my neck go before he got too much. Although, it still hurts. It wasn't as bad as the last time I was attacked. That blood-sucker must have wanted to inflict as much pain as possible. I'm just glad you all arrived when you did and were able to tear him apart."

Sighing, I tried to push out the memory from over six months ago when I first met Rico and his pack.

Jimmie came in with a bowl of wonton soup and a cup of tea for Damien. He also had a teapot on his tray and refilled my tea.

"Thanks, Jimmie." I took a sip of my full cup of green tea and sighed. It was the best tea, besides my rose tea, of course.

"What did you do to trick the vamp?" Damien asked before taking a sip of his tea.

Jimmie's eyes widened. "You were attacked by a vampire and survived? Mad props, Jenna."

"I told him I wanted to jump his bones, if he let my neck go." I blinked and watched as Damien choked on the tea he was drinking.

Jimmie busted up laughing. "Oh, Jenna. I always knew you were my kind of girl! Free wonton soup for you!"

"YOU.TOLD.HIM.WHAT?"

I froze when I heard Rico's voice. If he was angry earlier, I had no clue what this emotion was. Something primal inside of me knew to cower. Slowly, I turned around and could swear steam was coming off Rico's head.

The next thing I knew, a wolf was standing right in front of me and sniffing my body.

"Jenna, don't move. He won't hurt you. Just sit there and let him get his fury under control." Damien stood up holding his hands in the air, like it was a stick-up.

"Rico, she's fine. She tricked the vamp into getting his fangs off her neck, nothing more. Calm down and shift back. Let her tell you the whole story." I had never heard Damien talk so softly or comfortingly before.

Should I be afraid? I wasn't really sure. My head knew that Rico would never do a thing to harm me. But something inside of me was screaming to get away from the scary wolf who had its nose on my neck.

Rico continued to sniff my entire body. Before he was even half-way done checking me out, he sneezed. Most likely the stench of vampire, or the alley, caused an allergic reaction. Couldn't be sure which one. Once he was done, he magically shifted back into the human man I knew.

Rico was wearing blue jeans and a tight black t-shirt which showed off his gigantic biceps. Despite his yummy arms, it was a relief to know whenever he, or the others, shifted they would be fully clothed.

Since their shift originated from magic, anything they had on their body when they changed forms was held some-where else. Maybe another dimension? I'd have to think about it more later. Right now, I needed to deal with Rico's grumpy face.

Taking a deep breath Rico asked, "What happened? Don't leave anything out."

I looked between the three men in the room and bit my lower lip.

"Well, I had placed an order with Jimmie. We order at least once a week from him. Never has there been an issue with walking here. It's only about five blocks from home. Usually, there are a lot of people on the streets and in the alleys. I guess the pending hurricane has sent people packing already." I shrugged. Most residents didn't bother leaving the city unless the storm was predicted to be over a category 1. We were all used to them.

Sighing, I thought back to how it all happened. "I'm not really sure where the vamp came from, but he grabbed me and dragged me into the alley as I was walking by."

Looking at Rico I said, "Thank you so much for the training you have given me over the past six months. I don't think I could have walked away from that, if you hadn't trained me so well."

I put my hand on Rico's forearm and gave him a light squeeze. He took the chair next to mine and sat down.

"Your training isn't finished. It's only just begun." The heat in Rico's gaze sent chills down my spine. The kind where I wondered what pain and torture the beast would come up with next.

The day after Acadia was brought home safely, Rico insisted all of us begin training. I have three adopted sisters, we are known best as the Voodoo Dolls. We run a voodoo doll shop in the French Quarter. We're also a local indie rock band on our way to becoming famous, or infamous. Depending on what happens next.

He was a terrific teacher. However, for the first few months, I was covered in bruises after every session with him. So were my sisters. We all tried to get Damien or Joseph to train us, but Rico wouldn't hear of it. At least seventy-five percent of the time, we were trained by Rico. The only time someone else worked with us was when more bodies were needed, or Rico was called away on a mission.

"Don't change the subject. What happened?" Rico practically growled.

Okay, he wasn't calming down. Maybe he needed some soup or tea?

"Jimmie, I think Rico might need some wontons and any type of calming tea you have." I licked my lips and tried very hard not to show Rico my fear. It would only upset him if he knew he was the cause.

Jimmie went to the kitchen to get Rico something to eat and drink.

"Rico, chill man. She's fine. Her training saved her, and

maybe a little bit of her snarky attitude helped." Damien was a lifesaver!

He was also pretty smart and handsome. I couldn't understand why he didn't have a girlfriend. The guy was built like a wrestler and looked like a movie star. I had seen him without his shirt on once and almost drooled. The man had a chiseled chest and rock hard abs to die for.

Like most of the wolf-shifters, he had thick, brown hair. He kept it just above his collar. I always wondered if their human hair length determined how long the hair on their coat was, when they were shifted.

"Jenna, forgive me. I'm not angry with you, only with myself for not being there to protect you." Rico looked down at his hands, which were balled up on the table.

"Rico, you can't be with me at all times. You have a pack to run as well as a business. Your training worked. I might be a little bit injured, but overall, I'm fine. He got very little blood from me, and in the end, he was the one who died. Not me." I knew Rico was going to be glued to me every night for at least the next few weeks after this. He was always so overprotective of me.

Plus, the training was going to be brutal. Epsom salt baths for the next month, at least.

"Shh, turn up the volume on the TV. They're talking about all of the missing co-eds. Do you guys know anything about this?" I had seen a few reports of freshman from the local college going missing.

The college said the girls had just up and left. They did leave notes for their roommates and even took their stuff. The current thought was it was too tough on them, and they left. So far, none of them have been reported missing by family back home. I wondered if it was something else, like maybe vampires luring them away to life as an acolyte.

"This just in. Another freshman girl has gone missing from the University of New Orleans. Stephanie Cervantes was last seen leaving class almost one week ago. She has long brown hair and is five feet four inches tall. She was last seen wearing blue jeans and a UNO baseball team shirt."

"Her roommate never reported her missing. It wasn't until the dorm monitor noticed that Stephanie's personal belongings were gone that an official report was filed."

"Stephanie's roommate had a note and gave it to school officials, but we have received a copy. It stated classes were too tough, and Stephanie was going to travel around and see the country before going home. This is the fourth such note we have heard of this semester. School officials have assured us this isn't uncommon for freshman to take off in the middle of their first term without a good reason."

"Stay tuned for more on this developing story. Sasha, back to you for an update on the hurricane." Sasha came on with her fake boobs and low cut dress which only served to distract the men from her report. A report which was usually wrong.

"Alright, you can turn it back down. She's probably going to spout some more nonsense." I shook my head and laughed at the open-mouthed stare on Jimmie's face.

Jimmy was happily married, but it didn't stop him from being under Sasha's charms.

It wasn't long before ten more wolf-shifters showed up. For a place that was supposed to be closed, Uncle Wong's was pretty busy.

"*J*enna, please don't go anywhere at night alone anymore." Rico walked me home after we'd all ate.

I wished I had brought the van. The rain started coming down much harder than before. Maybe Sasha was right after all.

After only two blocks, the winds picked up as well. With the rain coming down and the gusts at least ten miles an hour, I would be drenched by the time I arrived back home.

"Rico, I can't promise that. We're training to fight for a reason. I don't want to let the vampires own the night. If they aren't going to play by the rules, then I'm going to kill them. Plain and simple." There was no way I would take the coward's way out.

"Vampires are no better than terrorists. You can't let them win. I'm standing up for all humans. I bet once we start killing a few, the queen will make sure they play by the rules. Your council will make sure, right?"

"Jenna, the council has other things to worry about right now. A few rogue vamps who attack women walking alone at night are not on their radar. Not even a little bit. No matter what I say." Rico pulled me to a stop next to him.

"If you want, you and your sisters can come out to my place and ride out the storm. We have a few boats, in case the levy's break again, or the water level gets too high. Either way, I think it might be safer if you all stayed with us for the next couple of days." Rico swept a wet, stringy lock of hair out of my eyes.

A few months back, Rico had asked me out. I shot him down. The timing was all off. Since then, he's backed off. I wasn't sure if it was what I wanted or not.

Times like this, when it was just the two of us and he

touched me, was when I wondered if I made the wrong choice. He had to know my heart was beating a mile a minute. Part of me wanted him to kiss me and another just wanted a long soak in a hot bath. Alone.

"Thank you for the offer, but what about our store? We have to get everything up off the ground floor before we can think about leaving. I would feel better if we could bring our instruments with us. Will they be safe at your place?" Our instruments were one of our most treasured possessions.

We could lose the store and be okay. The loss of our guitars and drums would kill us.

"Of course. You can bring anything you want. How about I come over tomorrow with one of our vans and help you pack up? I can even have a few of the wolves help clear out your store, just in case the water level rises too high."

We lived below sea level. Hurricanes and tropical storms hit all the time. We had a system for when the weather turned bad, like it would be in the next day or two.

"Thanks, Rico. That would be wonderful. Now, can I get home and take a hot bath? I really want this stench off of me." I laughed.

He had to smell me. Not to mention the fact of how I must look like a drowned cat by now. I only had a light hoodie on; which did nothing to keep the rain off my clothes and hair.

"Of course. I'll walk you home and then go take care of the trash you left behind." Rico winked and walked ahead of me.

3

JENNA

"*W*here have you been? I've been trying to call you for the past hour!" Kat stopped yelling and stared at me when I walked in the door. Rico was right behind me.

Sam ran and almost tackled me with her hug. "Oh! My! Gosh! Are you alright? What happened? Why didn't you call us? We were worried sick!"

"I'm fine. Or least I will be once I take a long soak in the tub. Do we still have any Epsom salt? Or that lavender rose bath ball? I'll probably need both." I motioned for Rico to come in and shut the door.

"Once you have done that, don't forget to clean off with rubbing alcohol." Kat's nose twitched when she got close enough to smell me.

Sam pushed me back. "Sorry, but can you at least go shower now? Then tell us what happened?" Her eyes were watering.

Great, I didn't realize my scent was enough to invoke a physical response. Why didn't anyone tell me it was so bad before? Maybe Rico's sneezes should have been enough to warn me. Oh well.

"Thanks, what a way to be welcomed home. Fine. I'll go shower really quickly and get the vamp scent off with the rubbing alcohol. Once I've told you all the story, then I'm taking a long bath. Maybe two." I rubbed my neck where the idiot vamp bit me and walked to the bathroom leaving Rico to field their questions.

*

*V*ampires were predators, the type who loved to steal from other vamps. They left a scent on their human acolytes to tell other blood-suckers to stay away. Rogue vamps were attracted by the scent of other vampires. Kat learned a long time ago to cover the scent by using rubbing alcohol.

Showering with rubbing alcohol wasn't something I normally did. "Ouch!" Rubbing alcohol stings on open wounds.

Thank goodness for Band-Aids and Neosporin. I lathered the gel on my bite marks and covered them up with a Band-Aid after I dressed.

Towel drying my hair as I walked into the living room, I called out, "Did Rico tell you I killed my first vamp tonight? All by myself too!"

"He also told us you were looking to get in bed with that vamp. Really, Jenna. You should know better than to play house with a blood-sucker!" Sam shook her head while stifling a laugh.

"Ha, ha!" I looked around the room. "Where's Rico?"

"He said something about needing to run off some steam? What happened? He said he would be back in the morning to help us pack. What does that mean?" Kat stood in front of the stove while a teapot simmered.

"Um, I agreed we would all go to his place tomorrow to sit out the storm. Looks like it's going to be a cat 2." Chewing on my lower lip, I wondered how much work we had before us.

"Yeah, we heard. We started clearing out the floor downstairs, just in case. We aren't done though. There is still at least five hours of work to be done. You should probably get some sleep and help with the rest early in the morning." Kat poured me a hot cup of my favorite rose tea.

"I don't see why we have to evacuate, it's only a cat 2. We can totally weather the storm right here, above our shop, like we normally do." Indie rolled her eyes.

It was a bit much to evacuate for this storm.

"I think it will be good for Rico. Plus, they have an awesome game room." Yes, I was using the wolf pack for their toys.

My sisters stopped what they were doing and looked to Sam. We all laughed. Sam had a crush on one of the guys in Rico's pack. It was also going to be a chance for Sam and Kyrie to spend more time together.

Sam came up and hugged me. "That's much better! I don't smell the rubbing alcohol. Did you use it?"

"Yes, and I covered my body in lavender lotion. Hopefully, I'll be able to sleep. If I can't sleep, I'll get up and start packing. I can always sleep once we're at Rico's." The pack all lived together in a sort of commune outside of town.

It was safer for them to stick together, and they had a fantastic set up! I actually couldn't wait to get there and relax while waiting out the storm. Some of the guys were into gaming so they have a game room filled with pinball machines and some of the old arcade games from before I was born.

"Alright, tell us what happened. Rico left right after saying you told the vamp you would jump his bones. What was that all about?" Indie laughed when she sat on the sofa.

"That was just to get his fangs off me. He had this vision of us playing Buffy and Spike, so I went along with it in hopes of distracting him. It worked." I shivered thinking about his fangs on my neck.

"I don't understand how acolytes can enjoy the feeding. I know that guy from earlier this year was rough because he wanted to kill me. However, tonight when Derek fed off me, it hurt. Like really hurt! Not as bad as before but still. How can anyone enjoy it?" Sticking my tongue out, I visibly shivered with the image of a vamp on my neck in my mind.

"It seems that a vampire can be very gentle and seductive when he wants. Acolytes get a sexual high from the feeding, which is why they stick around and let the vampires treat them as nothing more than walking, talking, blood banks." Kat had an "in" with an ostracized vampire.

"I'm not speaking from experience, 'cuz as you know, vamps don't like my blood. I wish I knew who my birth parents were now. I'd love to know how I have wolf-shifter blood but can't shift." Kat had a mixed heritage.

We never even knew it until a vamp attacked her a few years back.

Ivan saved her and told her she had shifter-blood. The vamp who attacked her said she had bad blood, so Ivan tasted it. She always denies it, but I know they have had a romantic on-again off-again relationship since they first met.

"Well, I hope I never have fangs on me again. This has just made me want to work even harder to learn to fight. I wonder if there is any magic we can get? I know I'm not a witch, but isn't there some sort of charm we can buy from witches to help protect us?" I knew Rico had a charm he never took off. It hung around his neck.

Indie scrunched her forehead and said, "We might, but I think that's a question for Joseph. He seems to have friends in the magical community. I highly doubt anyone would sell us anything. I'll see what I can find out once we get to the pack's place."

"About that, Rico said he would send some of his guys over in the morning to help us pack up the store and our van. He said we can take our instruments with us, and he can keep them safe if the levy's fail. They have boats for times like this." Yawning, I rubbed my face.

It seemed I might be able to sleep after all. "Look, I'm really exhausted. How about I tell you the tale come morning? While we're packing up the store?"

"Sure, get some sleep. The important thing is you're alright, and the vamp is dead." Sam gave me a hug before sending me to bed with a water bottle.

4

RICO

"Wake up!" I pounded on Jenna's door.

I couldn't believe these girls were still sleeping. The storm was still headed this way, and I wanted them all packed up and safely at my compound before it hit hard. The rain was already coming down in buckets.

"Come on, lazy bones! Time to get up and get packing!" I continued to pound.

"Hey, we're down here, dingle berry! We've been up since before the sun." Jenna came out from the store's back door.

"I'm surprised you're already up. I would have thought you would want to sleep in after last night." Walking down the stairs, I eyed Jenna up and down.

She looked tired, but in good spirits. There was a nice smile on her red face. I could tell she was working hard already. It was just past eight in the morning, and we didn't have much time left before the brunt of the storm hit.

Today, the forecasters said it could be a tropical storm, but they were still tracking it as a category 2 hurricane. Current time to landfall was just after one this afternoon.

"I figured I could sleep when we got to your place today. This was more important. Plus, I had nightmares." The storm developing in her eyes told me her shrug was a lie.

I knew Jenna well enough to know when she was trying to look like something wasn't bothering her, but was actually hurting. She was a strong and capable woman. I wish she would let me take care of her. She made it clear a few months ago how she felt. Although, sometimes I wondered if maybe she's starting to come around.

Now wasn't the time to think romantically. Now was the time to help her and her sisters pack up their store and get them to higher ground. At least, higher than the French Quarter.

"I'm sorry. Do you want to talk about it? Killing your first vamp is pretty huge. I'm not surprised you had bad dreams." Walking to her, I held out my arms for a hug.

Surprisingly, she walked right into my hug. I held her tight while we both said nothing. My head knew this was more about comfort than attraction, but my heart was soaring with the possibilities.

Pulling back, she looked me in the eyes and gave me a tentative smile. "Thanks, Rico. I think I needed that. Maybe we can talk once we're settled at your compound. Right now, I need to get my butt in gear and finish the packing. We're almost done, maybe another hour, and we can safely leave the store."

"Perfect. I have a van coming your way any minute now." I looked over my shoulder to see our van pulling in.

"Speak of the devil. Joseph and Luke are here to help as well." I waved the guys over once they parked.

"Come on, the girls are almost done. Looks like they were up before the crack of dawn getting ready for today." I high-fived Joseph as he walked past me in his rain gear.

"Jenna, good to see you doing so well. Damien told me all about your adventure last night. I think the pack would like to hear your version once we all get settled." Joseph was always asking everyone about their fights with vamps or witches.

He seemed to be writing it all up. I wasn't sure if he was preparing to write a book about it or just for the pack's history. Either way, it was a good idea to keep this info written down for the future generations.

"Sure, it's probably a good thing to talk about. Hopefully, it will help to get the creepiness out of my system. I'm still having a tough time thinking about it all. Especially the bite, and how he seemed to enjoy it." Jenna visibly shivered.

My instincts screamed at me to wrap my arms around her and tell her it was going to be alright.

"Jenna, I think I know a few things that might help you get a good night's sleep tonight. Once we're settled, and you have told everyone your story, we should take a walk." I rubbed her back and gave her a half smile.

She returned the smile and turned around without a word. When she walked back inside the store, I wasn't sure if that was a yes or no to my offer of help.

⁂

It took less than thirty minutes to finish preparing the store for the coming hurricane and possible damage. These girls really did have a great system for packing up. They have probably had way too many opportunities to practice.

If you didn't pack up at least the lower half of your store, then products were damaged every year. I had seen it too many times with store owners who were new to NOLA. We saw several storms a year that could cause a flood at the very least.

Those who grew up here knew the drill. Even if the city didn't flood, it was best to be prepared. The Boy Scouts motto was right on, *always be prepared*.

"I gotta say, I'm impressed with how organized you ladies are. You've got it down to a science. How many times a year do you do this?" I was driving their van, packed with their personal gear and the band's equipment, while Joseph drove our van packed with some of their more expensive items.

"We grew up doing this. I think we can all do it in our sleep now, right girls?" Kat was the matriarch of the group. She was only a couple years older than the rest, but she had taken on the motherly role when their adopted parents died. She took very good care of her adopted sisters.

"Sam, Kyrie's looking forward to challenging you on Call of Duty and Assassin's Creed. I hope you're up for it." I chuckled thinking about how the next few days might go.

I had no doubt Sam would be in heaven playing video games with Kyrie or any of the younger guys in my pack. However, Sam and Kyrie seemed to get along much better than anyone else did. Maybe these next few days would help him to get over his fear of rejection and finally ask her out.

And maybe, just maybe, I might as well.

"Wow, the roads are packed! It's a good thing we left early." Jenna was sitting in the front with me, and her sisters were in the back bench seat. Behind them was all of the stuff they were able to fit into their van.

"I hope we make it back to the compound before the hurricane hits." Just then the rain began to pelt our windows hard. It was as though someone turned on a spigot.

I wondered how long before the winds got above forty miles an hour as I gazed into the black, storm clouds.

"Nice going. Way to jinx us, Rico! I just hope we don't get stuck out here." Kat sure had a way with words.

We inched our way along the highway with rain coming down in sheets, and the wind whistled all around us.

"Do you think we'll be able to make it? Will the vans stand up to this beating?" Jenna looked out the window.

"As long as the winds don't get much worse, we should be able to weather this ride home. Both vans are loaded down pretty well, so it should help us to stay upright. It just means we have to drive slower, along with everyone else on the road." I looked at my speedometer, we were only doing thirty miles an hour.

"Whoa! What was that?" Indie screamed from the back.

Something had hit the roof of the van creating a loud thumping noise. We skidded off the side of the road, but I was able to get control back and get us up on the blacktop again.

"Was that a tree?" Kat asked.

Jenna turned in her seat and looked through the back windows of the van. "I think it was. We're lucky it went over the top and didn't go through the windshield."

hanks to the traffic, the wind, and the rain, it took us an extra hour to get home. It was a good thing we'd left when we did because the levies were on their way to overflowing. When we walked into the compound, all the TV's were tuned to the weather channel. Not the local NOLA one, but the national one.

We didn't have any more problems after the tree passed

us, thankfully. Just lots of rain and a few gusts which made it difficult to keep the van on the road, but we made it.

The wind was making a mess of our compound already. It was a good thing we were able to unload the vans so quickly. Winds had to be gusting over fifty miles an hour already. I hated to see what it would have been like once the gusts reached fifty if we were still on the road. Those wind speeds could have easily toppled our vans since they were riding so high.

"I don't know why they are still in town! Look at that guy! He's got his slickers on, but you know he's drenched straight through to the bone. If he's not careful, he's gonna be stuck in town and not be able to get out before the worst of it hits." Damien was watching the news along with most of my pack.

Another pack member commented, "Those winds are too strong for a regular human. If he doesn't move to higher ground, he's going to be picked up on one of those gusts and thrown all over. The winds there have to be close to sixty miles an hour now."

"Hey, can we get some help to unload? It'll go quicker the more hands we have." I knew my pack would help, even if they wanted to stay glued to the TV. They were always looking for ways to help, especially when pretty girls were involved.

"Sure!"

"You bet."

"Always willing to lend a helping hand."

"Are the Dolls here? I'll help!" Kyrie had been anxiously awaiting Sam's presence.

All of the men in the pack lounge got up to help. Each person only needed to make one trip to get both vans unpacked.

"I was thinking I would set the girls up in the meeting room. We can put their belongings in the room with them. Can someone get me four rollaways? I don't want them sleeping on the ground." I had put some thought into where the girls would sleep.

I knew I couldn't have them in my house, even if I felt that was the safest place for them. The next best place was the pack lounge, even if it was the busiest.

"Sure thing, boss." Luke took off with Brandon to grab the rollaway mattresses.

"Come on. Follow me with your suitcases, and I'll show you where you can stow it all." I waved for the girls to follow me down a narrow hallway.

"The women's restroom is to your left. It has a shower but, sorry no bathtub." I nodded toward it as we walked past.

"You saw the community kitchen when we walked in this building. Sorry, but it's open 24/7 to the entire pack. I'll put the word out you're sleeping here, but with the storm, I expect most of the pack to hang out here watching the TV. We have satellite here. Most of the homes on the compound only have an HD antennae to get the local stations." I was carrying four of their suitcases, and they each carried two. It was mind-boggling how much clothing they needed for just a few days.

"How many outfit changes do you go through over the course of one storm?" I chuckled as we walked into the large, oblong conference room.

There was a large wooden table that took up over half of the room, but we could move it to the side in order to open up some space. The chairs would most likely need to be rolled out to the main room anyways, what with all of the pack members who'll make their way here shortly.

"Hey, it's not all clothes in those suitcases! We brought supplies to make more voodoo dolls and even a few potions. That is, if you don't mind me using your kitchen to brew a few ingredients?" Jenna dropped her suitcases on the table making a loud clunking noise which led me to believe they were heavier than they looked.

"Feel free to keep your suitcases on the table, and I'll get the boys to take the chairs out for you." I put the four cases I carried on the conference table before pushing it to the far corner, opening up just enough space to fit four rollaways. It would be snug, but I doubted they would spend much time in here when they were awake.

"Thanks, Rico! We actually do need to change clothes already. Just bringing our stuff inside got us all soaked to the bones." Jenna was dripping wet, as were her sisters.

I didn't even notice. Living out here, you get used to wet wolves tracking in all sorts of mud and water.

Man, I hoped the storm wasn't bad. I would much rather spend this time getting closer to Jenna or even training her. That was actually a great idea. Since they were all stuck here for a few days, training them to fight would be a fantastic way to spend the time. Better than staying glued to the boobtube.

5

RICO

"*J*enna, I let the kitchen staff know you might be doing a few chemistry experiments while you're here. They're fine with it. Just be sure to clean up after yourself. If you have any questions, ReeAnna will be able to help you out." When Jenna walked into the room my eyes trailed right to her, even though I was very focused on the weather report.

"Now for the latest from the French Quarter of Louisiana where Hurricane Gerttie is getting ready fuɪ landfall." The weather anchor introduced the same guy from earlier, only this time it looked like he had moved to a safer part of town. At least he wasn't standing right next to Lake Pontchartrain this time.

Everyone turned their attention back to the seventy-inch flat screen on the wall. "Thank you, Lisa. As you can see, the rain is coming in hard. Along with the wind. Wind gusts have been tracked up to one hundred miles an hour, but they weren't sustained gusts. Some trees have already been toppled onto a few cars. Power lines have been brought down just from the sheer force of the rain and winds."

"We expect this to be a category 2 when it hits within the next hour. Our forecasters believe it will lose steam once it clears a path right next to New Orleans. The current models show the trajectory to hit south of the city and head out to the west where it should quickly turn into a tropical storm."

"If you haven't already left town, you are most likely stuck as the roads are washed out, and the winds will make it almost impossible to stay on the roads that aren't already underwater. Please get to the nearest hurricane shelter. I wouldn't try riding this out at home, unless you also have a boat sitting on your roof, like this guy here." The TV image changed to a guy sitting on his roof with a zodiac boat and what looked to be a case of beer.

The idiot was actually going to ride out the storm sitting in a boat on his roof drinking beer. I didn't know what would kill him first, the rain and winds, or the drinking. If he keeps drinking he won't be able to get himself to safety. Some people. Really, where do they get these asinine ideas?

The images changed again to a street near the lake. It was covered in water and debris. There wasn't a weatherman visible in this shot. It must have been a camera they installed before the weather turned too bad.

"Greg, can you zoom in on the Pontchartrain camera? There looks to be a person on the ground." I watched with rapt attention as the camera zoomed away from the surrounding storm and into the murky water running along the road next to one of the clubs I recognized, The Blue Bayou.

Everyone in the room gasped at the same time as the weather man did. "Lisa, I think that's a body on the ground. Are you seeing this? Do we already have a fatality?"

The image quickly went back to the woman wearing a pink dress in a warm and comfortable studio somewhere far from here, probably in New York or LA. Her eyes were wide, and she cleared her throat before reading from the teleprompter.

"Well, as you can see, it's very dangerous in New Orleans at the moment. Please remember to stay safe and don't go near running water or downed power lines. That's a surefire way to injure yourself or worse. And now a word from our sponsors." The commercials started and everyone in the room began questioning what they saw.

"Rico, I know it was a dead body, but it looked like she had vampire bites on her neck." Jenna sat next to me on the leather couch.

"We can't know that for sure. She was probably in the clutches of a gator, those could have been alligator bites on her neck." I really hoped those were gator bites on her neck. The young woman, or at least it looked like it was a young woman, was missing an arm and a few chunks were taken out of her torso as well.

Other than those missing freshman, who left notes and cleaned out their dorm rooms, there weren't any other missing women I knew of. If those were vampire bites, it meant we had more rogue vamps in the area.

Once this storm cleared out, and the roads were open again, I'd have Joseph head into the county morgue and see what he could find out. Joseph was friends with a few of the pathologists in our local morgue. They usually called him when they found anything that looked like paranormals may have been involved.

They would never call it paranormal activity. The authorities would just claim it's above their paygrade, or they don't have the tools to investigate a particular body properly.

"Jenna, are you ready to tell everyone what happened

last night? I know the guys would love to hear how you kicked that vamps butt and sent him back to hell!" Joseph wasn't going to let her get out of this.

It would be good for her. The more she talked about it, the easier it would be to get past it. Bottling up pain was never a good idea.

"Do you really want to know? I mean, you guys kill bad guys all the time, don't you?" Jenna was cute when she scrunched her nose and looked all innocent.

"Hellz yeah, we do!"

"You know it!"

"Come on, don't be so shy. You know you want to tell us how you sent that blood-sucker to its death!" Damien had heard the story already, not sure why he was getting into this.

"Actually, we don't kill too often. Only when a vampire has gone rogue do we have the right to kill. Or the occasional werewolf who can't be stopped." It was almost always my call if someone could kill a para or not.

"Too bad we can't kill the witches! They seem to be the ones behind most of the issues." Luke exclaimed.

"They certainly don't help matters, but with their council located here, we have to report those who are out of line and let their leadership deal with them. Usually, the punishment fits the crime, if they are caught." I knew for a fact a few got off easy.

For the most part, they did get punished. A few even had their magical abilities taken from them. Although, that punishment was as rare as death.

"The fight didn't last too long, I don't think. Maybe twenty minutes? The toughest part was making sure to stab him in the heart. It took two tries before I got him. Thankfully, I had a second stake in my boot. Also, they're kinda dumb." Jenna gave a nervous laugh before telling us all her story.

I hated hearing the part about that demon spawn's lips on her.

"Wait, you mean to tell me he was going to drain you dry, if you didn't agree to be his acolyte?" Joseph was in note-taking mode.

"Yup. I used his desire to trick him into letting my neck go. If I didn't, he would have drank too much of my blood, and I never would have gotten away. I guess pop culture saved my life last night." Jenna looked at me.

She knew I was close to changing again. My skin was shimmering, and the pack all looked at me with wide eyes.

"Rico, let's take a walk. I think we should check on the roof. Make sure those gusts aren't taking it all off." Damien stood up and moved closer to me.

Jenna should have moved further away from me, but instead, she did the opposite.

"Rico, it's alright. I'm right here. He wasn't going to get me as an acolyte. You've trained me too well for that. I promise. I'll work even harder so I'm never in a situation like that again." When Jenna put her hand on my shoulder, I felt the anger dissipate. The storm outside matched the storm inside until she touched me.

After I took a few calming breaths, I noticed the tension in the room had dropped away. My pack members knew I would never hurt anyone, but if someone was too close when I shifted, they might get injured. I think that's the only reason I didn't shift this time. Jenna was right next to me. My wolf would never allow any harm to come to her, no matter how angry I was.

"Jenna, it might be best for you to back up if I'm ever too angry to control my change. You know I would never intentionally harm you, but if you're too close when I begin to change, you could be injured. I wouldn't be able to forgive myself if I hurt you in the process." I took ahold of her hand and squeezed it.

"Rico, I know your wolf would never hurt me. I also know my touch can calm you when you're too worked up to calm yourself. I'm not afraid of you."

"You were last night when I shifted. I smelled it on you."

"That's only because of what I had already been through. You probably would have smelled the fear on me even if you hadn't changed like that." Jenna was probably right.

"Let's take a walk. I think we need to talk." I stood up and held my hand out to her.

"Um, Rico. There's a hurricane outside. I don't think we should go out there."

I shook my head and realized what a dumb suggestion that was. "Alright, how about we have a chat in my office? It's just down the hall."

Jenna smiled as she stood up. "Sure, that would be great."

6

JENNA

"*R*ico, earlier you said you had a way to help me sleep better? Does it involve magic?"

"Come here." Rico reached out to hug me, and I accepted.

Sighing, I wrapped my arms around him. "I don't think this is going to help me sleep tonight." I couldn't help but giggle.

His arms were so strong and safe. I couldn't help but compare him to the vampire from last night. Which wasn't fair. Rico was nothing like that disgusting spawn of the devil. Rico was...gentle. He would never force himself on me or hurt me. Why couldn't I open myself up to him?

"No, but it will help me." He had such a nice deep laugh.

I pulled back and smiled at him. "Alright, what's this life changing advice you have for me?"

I looked up to the roof when I heard a thunk. The winds were tossing around debris, and we'd probably be hearing noises like that all night long.

"You need to talk through it all, including how you felt. As much as I want to be that person, you saw how I reacted out there. I think you should talk to Joseph, or whoever you feel comfortable with. Just be sure to be honest with him and yourself." This wasn't what I expected to hear from Rico.

"Really? You want me to open up with someone other than you?"

"No, I want you to open up with me, but I know I can't handle it right now. Maybe in a few days I can. It's all too raw for me at the moment. I know it's not fair to you. As much as I want to put aside my anger, I can't." Rico sat down on the sofa in his office.

He patted the spot on the sofa next to him. "Seeing you injured and smelling him all over you last night...it brought out the animal in me. And I don't mean my wolf. If you hadn't killed him, I would have ran out of there and hunted him down, no matter how long it took."

"Thank you, Rico. I appreciate your protective nature, I do. It's just..." Stink! How do I explain this to him?

"It's just what? You can tell me. I promise I won't overreact." Rico could be so sweet.

I leaned in closer to him and put my hand on his cheek. My eyes roamed his face and landed on his lips. My heart beat increased as I licked my lips, wondering what it would be like to have his lips on mine. At that moment I wanted to kiss him, but did I want it because I wanted his lips to star in my dreams instead of Derek's in my nightmares?

Rico moved closer to me. "Jenna, is this what you want?"

His lips were so close to mine, I could feel his breath on my face.

"Hey, Rico. You might... Oh! Sorry man." Joseph had walked in before I could say anything.

I pulled away from Rico as my cheeks warmed.

"It's fine, Joseph. What's up?" Rico let me go when he stood up to greet his friend.

"Sorry, it can wait." Joseph backed up and was about to close the door when Damien walked up behind him.

"What's going on?" Rico walked to the door where two of his most trusted advisors had barged in on us.

"The news - you need to see this. Looks like we get to go hunting when the hurricane clears." Damien's eyes sparkled with excitement before he turned around and headed back out to the main room.

That guy loved nothing more than to pound on the bad guys. Looks like something had happened to give him a hunting license.

We all followed him down the narrow hall. These guys were so big they had to walk single file through here.

"Jenna! That girl we saw on the news earlier, she's the one who went missing! Stephanie, I think her name was." Indie looked up to me with wide eyes.

I put my hand over my mouth. "No! That means vampires, right? Or something else not normal?"

"We haven't had a full moon since she went missing, so it couldn't have been a werewolf. That only leaves vampires and witches. My money's on vamps. Did you see those bite marks on her neck? It didn't look like a gator did that, unless it was a baby." Luke stood up to let me sit on the couch next to my sisters.

"So what does this mean, exactly? Could all of the other girls who disappeared have something to do with blood-suckers?" I shivered hoping they didn't experience anything like what I did.

Kat asked, "Could it be just the one girl who went missing was caught up by a vampire on her way out of town?

No other bodies have shown up with vampire marks, have they?"

"I won't know until I talk to my friend at the morgue. I doubt he'll be in for at least two days. However, I'll give him a call tomorrow and see if he has any information at all," Joseph replied.

"Pack, it's time to work out. We have a lot of time before we can leave, and all four of The Voodoo Dolls are here. Let's run them through a series of workouts and teach them some more ways to kill a vampire." Rico turned off the TV and led us all out the back of the building.

That was an abrupt segue if ever I heard one. Was he trying to get our minds off the missing girls? Or the possibility of vampires?

Thank goodness they had a covered walkway from the main hall to their gym. Kat and Sam had to go and change into yoga pants. Indie and I already had them on. We both were more comfortable hanging out in our comfy clothes.

"*I* think I want to die! Come on! Please let me lay here until I can move." Rico and his pack worked all four of us hard!

The past four hours were spent sparring, doing sit-ups, push-ups, and things called burpees. When he first said the word, I thought he meant we were going to have a burping contest. A burpee is NOT a burp. Gas can be involved but not in a fun way.

It is a total body workout that makes me regret all the frappuccinos I ever had.

We would do a set of five burpees then spar a round or two, then a set of burpees and sparring. It was a never ending cycle of torture! I think I would rather fight a vampire.

"Come on, Jenna. This is going to help you strengthen your body and learn to push through any pain you have when fighting off something bigger or stronger than you are. Don't be a wimp." Damien was evil incarnate.

"Damien, we aren't in the same shape as you guys. Give us a break." I couldn't move, even if I wanted to.

Rico stood back watching and laughing, the jerk. "Alright, hit the showers, girls. Tomorrow morning be ready for more. I think we'll try working out in two hour shifts to see if you can handle more. I only have you here for a couple of days, so I'm going to get as much blood and sweat out of you all as I can."

"Ugh." Kat said it all.

The four of us stayed on the floor for a good fifteen minutes before anyone helped us up. Then we waddled like ducks all the way to the showers. I think I would have rather stayed in our apartment and battled the hurricane.

7

JENNA

"Ow! Do we really have to workout today?" Sam grumbled while she tried to get out of bed.

"No, we don't." I wasn't getting out of bed, unless it was for an Epsom salt bath.

The next day I couldn't stand up straight. Rico said he had a way to help me sleep, practically killing me with his work-out was the ticket. I slept for a straight ten hours. I doubted I moved once in my sleep.

"Girls, we have to do this. At least do some stretches to break down the lactic acid that's built up overnight." Kat was evil. She and Damien would make a great couple.

"I don't wanna," Indie grumbled.

"Ladies, it's time to get up. Breakfast is ready." Rico was outside our door trying to tempt us with food.

It worked.

"Is that bacon I smell?" Bacon could get me out of bed.

It seemed it would get all of us out of bed.

We must have been a sight. When we walked into the kitchen hunched over and waddling like old ducks, the room erupted into laughter.

"Ha, ha. This is what happens when normal humans try to keep up with wolf-shifters. Not a pleasant sight or feeling. I don't think we can workout today." I rubbed my back when I sat on the hard plastic chair at the table.

Thankfully, ReeAnna took pity on us and served us a wonderful smelling breakfast of bacon, eggs, and sourdough toast.

"Oh, is that coffee I smell?" I needed coffee almost as much as I needed air.

"Yes, do you want cream and sugar?" ReeAnna was a goddess.

She was close to six feet tall. I suspected all shifters had the height gene. Her heritage must have been Cajun because she had smooth, chocolate skin any woman would die for. She kept her hair wrapped up in a sort of colorful turban. She kinda reminded me of the stereotypical voodoo priestess, instead of a shifter.

"Please, and thank you. This all looks and smells so good." Sam picked up a slice of thick bacon. It looked to be cooked to perfection.

I had four pieces on my plate. It hurt to bring my arm up, but for bacon, I would endure the pain.

"Rico, I can't believe you did this to those poor girls! Shame on you!" ReeAnna slapped his shoulder with the back of her hand.

Something inside of me didn't like her touching him. He wasn't my man. Why did I care if she hit him? Maybe it was because I wanted to be the one who hit him? I just didn't have the strength to get up out of my chair.

"Ladies, I have a bathtub in my house. Once breakfast is over I'll take you over to soak. I think I have some soothing bath salts which should help some of your inflammation. I hate to say it, but you will need to do at least some stretches today so you can work out the kinks and lactic acid." ReeAnna was a woman after my own heart.

If she had bath salts, I would try stretching after a nice long soak.

"Thank you, ReeAnna.It's nice to know at least one person here has a heart." Indie looked to be in as much pain as I was. She was slowly bringing her fork to her mouth with a bite of egg, which fell off her fork before she could get it into her mouth.

Joseph sat next to Indie and helped her get some egg on her fork and into her mouth. "Thanks, but I think I can feed myself. I am a grown woman, you know."

"Oh, I know." Joseph stood up and walked out of the room.

"Indie, he was just trying to help. Don't be so rude." I picked up a slice of bacon and took a bite. "Mmm. That's perfection."

"How would you feel if Rico came over and started feeding you like a baby?" Indie needed more caffeine. She wasn't usually so touchy.

"Right now? I think I'd be fine. However, after I finished, he would probably get forked for putting me in this position." I was sitting next to Rico, and he spewed his coffee on his breakfast plate. Served him right.

He put his hands in the air after wiping his face. "Alright, alright. I get it. We over did it yesterday. I'm sorry. Really I am. How can we help?"

"For starters, you can help me get my eggs in my mouth. Then, you can slap some butter and jam on my toast. After that, I'll let you know." He wasn't getting out of this too easily.

"Do you have a masseuse on site?" Kat had the right idea.

8

JENNA

"Wow! Look at that rain! I can't believe it's still coming down so hard. Do you think we can go home tomorrow? I bet we have a lot of cleanup to do in the shop." The hurricane passed us by yesterday, thankfully!

Yesterday was a wasted day. None of us felt like moving. With the hurricane, it really didn't matter anyway. So we soaked in ReeAnna's tub with scented bath salts and stretched.

Rico offered to give me a massage, but it seemed to…intimate. I did let him massage my shoulders. Indie let Joseph massage hers, while Luke offered to rub Kat and Sam's shoulders. I noticed Kyrie wasn't too happy when Luke offered to help Sam. He narrowed his eyes and pursed his lips before stomping out of the room.

While I felt a bit better, I was bummed we couldn't leave yet. It was probably for the best since we were all still so sore.

There was some damage, but the levies held. Flooding wasn't too bad, according to the news service. Sasha said the rain should stop later today. I just hoped she was accurate, for a change.

"Once the roads open up, I'll take you ladies back. How about a light workout today? It would do your muscles some good." Rico was evil. There was no reason to get us to workout so soon, other than him being the devil incarnate.

Kat put her hand up to stop me. I was about to go off on him.

"We could use some sparring and a light warm up. By light, I really do mean light. No more of the shifter workout regimen for us. Please try to remember we are only human." Kat could deal with Rico and his need to torture us.

Didn't mean I was going to work out. When I walked through the main room, the big screen was on the news, of course.

"Hey, are they talking about the missing girls?" The image of our local news team drew my attention.

"Yes, someone looked into the other girls who were missing and none had checked in with family. The family thought they were just busy at school. This is looking to be a big deal." Luke was glued to the TV.

I sat down next to him on the couch. "So, you think it's vampire related?"

"Of course. However, it could be something else. Even though there are multiple girls missing, some could be just fine. Some could be acolytes. As hard as it is to believe, some women and men, actually choose that lifestyle. We can't do anything about it." Luke's eyes darkened as he spoke.

"Why would they do that? I don't get it. Is their regular, mundane life so horrible they have to choose a path that will only lead to an early death?" It made no sense, even if a bite could feel good.

This was not a good choice for anyone.

"I mean, I get it if someone is dying. They would want to have the chance at immortality if they could. I wouldn't, but I can understand someone else choosing that. Rico said some of the acolytes get chosen to become vamps." I think it was Rico who said it. Maybe it was Joseph?

"Yeah, sometimes it happens. More often than not, they just end up as dinner. I think the reason people choose that life is because of what they read in books and see in movies. Remember the one with the shimmering vampires who said they were vegetarians? After that movie came out, we had an influx of young women who wanted to be acolytes. Most of them are dead now." Luke shook his head.

"That's awful! But, I can see it. I romanticized them too after that movie. Not that I wanted to give up my life, but it would have been cool to date a vamp back then." I laughed at myself for thinking such thoughts now that I knew the truth.

"So, you were team vamp? Not team wolf?" Rico walked into the room and startled me.

I bit my lower lip. "Um, at the time? Yes. Now? Team wolf all the way! I just rewatched the series a few weeks back and wondered what I ever saw in the vampires. To be fair, now I know the truth, I'm seeing it all in a new light."

"Well, at least you can admit when you're wrong." Luke laughed and said, "Shh. They have more info on the missing girls."

Everyone in the room shut up quickly and turned their attention to the TV.

"We have confirmed with all of the parents of the missing girls. Only one of the five missing girls have checked in with her parents. Sadly, three of the missing girls were orphans and had no one to check in with. Our investigative team have determined there are at least four girls unaccounted for, not counting the one who was discovered when she washed up downtown during the hurricane. The local authorities will begin working with the University to discover what happened to the girls as soon as the roads clear up, and they can begin an official investigation. Keep tuned in for more on this emerging story."

"Wow, I wonder how many of those five were killed by vamps? I hope some are still alive." I rubbed my eyes and felt dampness on one of my fingers.

This story was hitting a little too close to home. Was Derek one of those responsible for any of the missing girls? Did killing him help any of them? I hoped so.

"Hold up! Since when has it been five missing girls? The last report I saw showed four girls." Indie narrowed her brows and silently counted on her fingers.

"Last night there was another report detailing all of the missing girls. They discovered another with a note similar to the others." I should have updated Indie after the news report.

To be honest, I was in too much pain to talk about it anymore. Those poor girls. I hadn't been held by vamps, but I have been attacked a couple of times. To imagine what they were going through only brought back horrendous memories for me.

"Joseph, have you been able to reach your contact in the morgue?" Rico questioned the alchemist when he walked into the room.

"Yes, he told me right before they were ordered to evacuate, a body came in with marks on her neck. There were multiple teeth marks. He was planning on calling me when he returned to the office." Joseph's face was white as a ghost.

"Multiple marks? Does it mean many vampires fed off her? Or does it mean whoever she served just fed many times?" It had to hurt. I couldn't fathom what she went through.

"It's hard to say. I need to know how fresh the marks are. Usually, a mark will heal in a day or two. Most likely, multiple vampires fed off her before killing her. She probably died with all of them sucking her dry at once. It's very common with a small group of rogue vamps to feed that way. They aren't good at taking turns or going slowly." Rico swallowed hard and sighed.

"That would have hurt, a lot, huh?" I looked at the hands in my lap and noticed a tear had fallen onto my arm.

Rico put his arm around my shoulder. "Hey, let's not speculate. Joseph will do his exam as soon as he can get to the morgue. If that body was picked up before the storm hit, there will probably be plenty of evidence on it to help us track down the killer. Or killers."

"Yeah, you're right. It's not good to think about the possibilities. I hope the roads are clear enough to drive on tomorrow." It was going to be a long day.

I know her!" I yelled out as I pointed to the screen. Later that evening, after dinner, we were all watching the news update regarding the missing girls.

"She came into our shop a couple of times before she went missing." I was mesmerized by her high school graduation photo the newscaster was showing.

Our local newsman, Trey Davis, was wearing his signature three piece suit and bowtie. I always liked his reports. Of all of the people on the news, he seemed the most genuine when he read the teleprompter.

"Melissa was a straight A student who graduated at the

top of her class. She came from a small town in Wyoming. She planned to study Hotel, Restaurant, and Tourism so she could return home to help her parents turn their small ranch into a working dude ranch. Her parents have not heard from her in over a month. The last time she phoned home, she sounded despondent. Her boyfriend had broken up with her via text message while she was in class."

"As soon as they heard about the hurricane they began calling her cell, which had been turned off, and reached out to Melissa's roommate. This was when they discovered their only daughter had gone missing. Melissa's roommate stated she left school just about two weeks ago." The image changed to a group of young women, one of which was a smiling Melissa.

"If you have seen Melissa, please call your local police or sheriffs' department. Stay tuned for more about Hurricane Gerttie and her path of destruction." Trey Davis said something about commercials, but I was too shocked to pay attention.

"Poor Melissa! She was so sweet. When she first came to the shop, she wanted to try a love potion to get her boyfriend back. When it didn't work, she wanted revenge. He had met another freshman. It seemed he was a senior who liked to hook up with as many new girls as he could." I remembered her sad, green eyes when she came in both times.

"I wonder if she chose to become an acolyte. Would a vamp use her breakup to lure her in?" My unfocused eyes stared at a blank wall.

"It's possible. We will begin looking for all of the girls tomorrow. I must warn you, if they chose to live with the vamps, we can't do anything for them. We can't even let their families know they are still alive. It's better to let them assume the girls died. They never leave the vampires once they choose that life. It's a lifelong commitment, no matter how short their lives may be." Joseph really knew how to cheer up a room.

Everyone looked at the ground, a few sighed. All were quiet until Rico broke the silence.

"I say it's time we have some fun. Let's get a video game competition going. Who wants to challenge me to Mario Cart?" Rico stood up rubbing his hands together.

A few people laughed.

Kyrie said, "Rico, you suck at video games."

"I know, but it's still fun. This gives you all a chance to beat me at something, for a change." Rico winked at me.

"I'll challenge you!" I stood up smiling, relishing a chance to cream him!

RICO

"**K**nock, knock." It was early the next day, and the roads were clear.

I knew the girls needed to get back to their store and start cleaning so they could open up again. Plus, I wanted to get into town with Joseph to see what we could find out about the two bodies in the morgue.

"What? Can't we sleep a bit longer?" Indie moaned.

"The roads are clear. Didn't you want to get home and start cleaning your shop?" I knew that would get them up. After their music, their shop was the second most important thing to them.

"Yes, we'll be up and ready in five minutes. Does ReeAnna need help with breakfast? Or is that bacon and coffee I smell?" Kat didn't know it, but I held a cup of fresh coffee and two pieces of hot bacon in my hands.

I had learned over the past couple of days, these were the two things that could get them moving in the morning. The promise of a hot cup 'o joe and our fresh bacon. We slaughtered our own pigs, so our bacon was fresher than anything you could get in the city. It also tasted much better.

Our butcher knew how to cure pork as well as how to cut the perfect slices for bacon. Not to mention we fed our pigs healthier slop than most pig farms.

"It's fresh bacon, coffee, and if you hurry, you can still get some waffles too." I heard rustling on the other side of the door.

Apparently, they liked waffles. Good to know.

I watched as four sets of droopy eyes began to open when they all sipped their first cup of coffee.

"Mmm, this is just what I needed." Sam closed her eyes and continued to sip her coffee in between bites of bacon and waffles.

"How much time do we have before you want to leave, Rico?" Indie asked.

"Can you be ready to go in thirty minutes?"

All four heads bobbed while they gobbled up their breakfast. At least they could eat without help today. I had to stifle my laugh as I recalled their first breakfast here two days ago, when they could barely move.

In hindsight, it was stupid of me to expect them to keep up with shifters. I just want them in fighting shape as fast as possible. It could mean the difference between surviving an attack...or not.

If anything happened to any of them, I would never forgive myself. They were family now. I knew most of my pack felt the same.

Most of my guys, and even a few of the women, volunteered to patrol near the Voodoo Doll House. Every night a different team would patrol the city looking for any paranormals who needed to be dealt with. They also paid close attention to Jenna and her sisters, making sure they were safe.

For the most part, everyone followed the rules. With

vampires, we usually had a few come through town wanting to sample the local flavors without permission. Those we were able to dispose of without getting into any trouble.

Since I met the Dolls, I have had this overwhelming sense of protectiveness for them. Several of the guys in my pack have crushes on the girls, and all who met them liked them instantly. It was hard not to like the girls. They were very nice and could even be funny at times.

Anyone who had the pleasure of seeing them perform in concert immediately wanted their CD's. Whenever we provided security for their gigs, the guys would all volunteer for that job. I doubted there was anyone in my pack who didn't like their music.

"Alright, I'll see you outside by the vans in thirty minutes. We can pack up and head to your store. Once we have you unloaded, I'll go with Joseph to the morgue and see what we can find out." I stood up carrying a fresh cup 'o joe and headed out to load up their instruments.

It was still raining outside, so I used a tarp to cover the equipment, while a few of us loaded it all up.

"At least it's a light rain today. Hopefully, it'll stop soon." Joseph loaded a guitar case covered in plastic, in the back of the van.

"Here's my suitcases. We have a few more inside to get. It's too bad we didn't have any free time to make up more voodoo dolls. We'll have to spend the next few evenings working on our inventory." Kat handed me two suitcases before she turned around and went back inside.

Indie walked out with two cases in her hands, but she wasn't wearing a jacket. The heavens opened up the moment she walked out and she was drenched before she even made it to the van.

"Ugh! Just my luck! Here, take my bags. I have to help

Kat with the rest. Hopefully, I can find my jacket some-
where." Indie shook herself off like a wolf before she walked
back inside.

I couldn't help but laugh. Her hair was stuck to her head,
and her bangs were poking her in the eyes. That poor thing
looked like a wet dog, but at least she didn't smell like
one, yet.

Right after she walked inside, the rain subsided. I
wondered if she had annoyed Mother Nature recently or
something. I knew she believed she had mad voodoo skills.
Could she have been trying something new? Maybe it was
just her bad luck?

Jenna came out dressed for the weather. She had on a
rain coat with the hood up over her bun. Even without
makeup on, she was beautiful. I almost killed Joseph for
interrupting us the other day. If he had waited just two
minutes, I think she might have kissed me. That moment
better come again and soon.

"Here, let me take that. Why don't you get inside before
the rain kicks back up." I took the suitcases from her hands
and put them inside the van Joseph was going to be driving.

Everyone else came out carrying bags and boxes we had
brought with us a few days ago. My guys were really great
when it came to helping.

"Hey, boss. I can come into town and help the girls
unpack, if you don't need me here for anything." Kyrie had
been spending a lot of time with Sam since they'd arrived.

"Sure. Hop in with Joseph. You'll have to stay in town
until we're ready to leave, which probably won't be until
late. You good with that?" I knew the public transportation
wouldn't be up today.

I also wanted to make sure the girls were settled before
the end of the day. Tomorrow, life would start going back to

normal. Or at least as much as it could. Their store would open back up and tourists, as well as locals, would most likely be visiting them again.

"Yup, Sam needs me to kick her butt again in Call of Duty. If we get the store put back together in time, I wanted to show her a couple of my more infamous moves." Kyrie needed to show her some moves alright, but video game moves shouldn't be on the top of his to-do list.

"Just make sure they don't go out after dark alone. These conditions are ripe for vampires to be out looking for a quick feed." I closed the back of the van door and nodded to the guys in the other van.

"ReeAnna gave us a box of fresh food. We'll be making dinner tonight. If you guys are still in town, feel free to join us. She gave us enough for a week of home-cooked meals." Indie said when she stepped into the back seat.

"Sounds like a plan. I doubt any restaurants will be open tonight anyway." I opened the driver's side door and jumped in.

"*B*reaking news." I caught the red banner which went across the TV screen indication something big was going on.

We had just finished putting the store back together.

"Turn up the TV. I want to hear what they have to say. I hope it's news about the missing girls." Kat went into the kitchen and grabbed a few Diet Cokes for everyone.

Normally, we didn't drink diet sodas because of Indie and her healthy habits. However, Diet Coke was one of the few items she didn't seem to mind. We all have our vices, this just happens to one of ours.

Sadly, the flooring in our shop would need some work. It looked like about an inch of water had gotten inside the store. I could see mildew starting to form on the bottom of the walls. We could clean most of it up, but the floor had seen several floods now, so it was time to replace it.

"This just in. Local authorities have confirmed two more local university girls have gone missing. Lisa and Gina were both last seen preparing to leave before the hurricane. They were supposed to join their dormmates at a predetermined evacuation facility, but they never made it. Neither girl knew the other one, as far as the university knows. Both wanted to drive their own cars packed with their gear to the evacuation center, and neither showed up.

"Local officials are working closely with the Red Cross to determine if they made it to a different site instead. Rest assured, everyone is working very hard to locate the missing girls. If you have any information, please contact your local police department. Here are the most recent photos of the missing girls."

On the screen, all of the girls who were currently listed as missing were shown. There were no similarities to any of them, other than being local UNO freshmen.

Gina was a pretty blonde girl, couldn't be any older than eighteen or nineteen. She had blue eyes and a sweet smile. She looked like the type of girl who helped people. Her eyes had a softness to them, she probably had lots of people who felt comfortable in her presence.

Lisa had beautiful auburn hair. Her green eyes sparkled, even in a picture. She looked to be about average height and the type of girl who did yoga. She was in yoga pants and flexing her arms in one of the images they showed on the news. Her face had a healthy glow to it, like she ate right and exercised. Too bad healthy habits couldn't save her.

Five of the girls were white, but even they all had different color hair and features. Then there were two black girls, and one looked to be Native American. None of these girls were tied to each other. It didn't make any sense.

"Kat, do you think it's the local vamps recruiting?" I opened my soda and after the fizz settled down I took a drink.

"If so, they are really drawing attention to themselves." Kat shook her head and looked at me.

Kyrie walked into the room, he had been setting up the video game system with Sam in her room. "It's probably a group of rogues, unless the local vampire queen is recruiting for the upcoming war. Although, if she is, she's in for a world of trouble. This is too obvious."

"What do you mean?" Sam was right behind Kyrie.

"Well, when the queen recruits, she usually picks people from various parts of the region. Most of the new recruits are usually acolytes who have earned the right to be changed. Then she'll send out some of her trusted vamps to get new recruits. They rarely grab two people from the same city." Kyrie went into the kitchen and grabbed a water bottle.

"If the war is coming, would she break tradition and grab as many girls as she could from here? Would the hurricane make it easier for her to get away with it?" Something didn't seem right. I doubted the queen would do this. Could it be something else was going on?

Without knocking, Rico walked in. "You really should keep your door locked at all times. You never know who might enter." He carried two big, brown take-out bags.

"Obviously, riff-raff will come in off the street if we don't keep the door locked. Thanks for the reminder." I shook my head and chuckled. I knew he was coming soon, which was why I had unlocked the door only five minutes ago.

"Whatcha got in the bag?" Indie bounced off the sofa and ran to grab the bags from Rico's hand.

"Uncle Wong's opened back up. He called to tell me he had a special order for us. Since most of my pack are still cleaning up the debris back home, I thought I'd bring it all over here and any wolves who do make it into town for patrol tonight could come by here. If that's alright with you?" Rico could be very generous, but there was no need to bring all of the food here. The wolves could just as easily head to Jimmie's to eat. He was up to something.

"Sure, but as you so kindly reminded me, the door will be locked." I walked over to the door and turned the dead-bolt and put the chain on the door. "You never know who might try to barge in on us."

Rico chuckled, and something inside of me warmed. I loved it when he laughed and smiled at me. *Stop thinking about him like that! He's just a friend.*

"Rico, your pack are always welcome here. Also, I think we will be just fine tonight. You don't need to send over any babysitters." Kat knew exactly what he was up to.

While I suspected, I wouldn't have called him out so blatantly, but Kat would. I had to laugh. She could always be depended on to say what was on her mind.

"Listen, after what happened with Jenna the other night, I'm going to be overprotective of you all. I would do the same with anyone in my pack. It's just who I am. Please, let me send over guys to keep an eye out for the next week. The vampires are always up to no good after a hurricane." Rico turned on his puppy dog eyes and pouted.

He was such a good manipulator. At least he used his charms for the right reasons.

"Fine, just make sure no one gets in our way. We have to work hard the rest of the week building back up our stock of voodoo dolls. After a big storm, there's always an influx of scorned women and even a few men. Something about the rains and the winds cause people to break up for the stupidest things and then want revenge." Indie held up a doll she had started working on.

It looked similar to one of her ex-boyfriends. These dolls sold the best, and we had a very hard time keeping them in stock.

"Is that Brian?" Rico pointed to the doll in question.

"Yup, he's my best seller. Looks rather like him too, even if I do say so myself. What do you think, Jenna?"

"Indie, you always get the face right. I can pick up any doll you make and name the ex you fashioned it after." Sometimes, we played a game where the dolls would get mixed up and put together. We would take turns pulling one out and naming the ex. It was kinda fun, when we were bored.

"Who do you think will be your next ex? Have we met him yet, Indie?" My money was on Joseph. He had the right look, and he even seemed interested in her.

"I don't know yet. I'm still considering all of my options at the moment. It's kinda fun just flirting and receiving all of the attention of an entire pack of hunky shifters right now." Indie always was a big flirt. I'm surprised she had agreed to be exclusive with so many guys already. I guess that's why she had so many exe's.

"I think we could all use a break from the drama of boyfriends right now." Kat sent me a pointed look.

I guess that was my queue to stay away from Rico. Message received. A boyfriend just wasn't something I had time for. With the storm and our music, we were going to be very busy for the next few weeks.

"When is our next gig, Kat?" We hadn't had a gig for a while and I was looking forward to the next one.

Kat was in talks with some of the local clubs to get us scheduled before Mardi Gras. Hopefully, we could get a few Mardi Gras gigs as well! Those always paid the best, and we sold out of our CD's whenever we performed during the holidays.

"I'm hoping for gigs every night during the Thanksgiving week. I have to give the managers some time to clean up their clubs before I start calling them again. We have one guaranteed gig at Thanksgiving and Mardi Gras, the Blue Bayou wants us back." Kat had been holding out on us.

"What? The Blue Bayou? Are you nuts? You do know what happened last time, right?" Rico was pacing the floor by the door and throwing his arms around.

I knew something went down, but it didn't affect us. "Rico, there were no issues for us. Those witches were just messing with you. I'm sure it'll be safe. Just bring more of your pack if you'll feel safer. Maybe even get us some of those protection charms you keep talking about?"

"Oh, I spoke with Joseph about them. He said, in a couple of days, he was going to see his witch friend, and he'd ask about getting us protection charms. He didn't seem to think it would be a problem. Where is he anyway? I thought you guys were together all day?" At least Indie had some good news.

"He's coming. I left him at Uncle Wong's. He was chatting with his friend from the morgue. They brought in another body today with questionable marks. I'll wait for him to tell you all about it." Rico calmed himself down by taking a few cleansing breaths before heading to the kitchen.

"Help yourself, girls. Jimmie packed up two large containers each of wonton soup, orange chicken, sweet and sour pork, pork-fried rice, and kung-pao chicken. There should be plenty of white rice too." Rico took the containers out of the bags and put them on the counter.

He had been here enough, he also knew where we kept the plates and silverware. It was odd having him pulling everything out in our kitchen for dinner. Although, somehow, comforting as well.

Halfway through dinner Joseph showed up.

"Hi, everyone. I hope you saved some of the fortune cookies for me. Those are my favorite!" Joseph grabbed a water bottle and looked through the bags for the cookies.

"Don't forget to eat the cookie before reading your fortune! Or else it won't come true," Indie yelled from the living room.

"No worries, I love eating these cookies. The anticipation of what my fortune will be makes the wait excruciating, but the cookie makes it worthwhile." Joseph cracked open his fortune cookie and pocketed the fortune before eating the cardboard.

I always thought the cookies tasted like flavored paper. My favorite were the almond cookies. Of course, I always ate my fortune cookie, if for no other reason than to get a fortune.

"Let's see. What's in my future?" Joseph had inhaled the cookie before pulling the small, white piece of paper out of his pocket.

"*You will meet your soulmate under the light of the next full moon.*"

"Huh, that's only three days from now. I wonder who I'll meet then?" Joseph looked directly at Indie who held his gaze.

This was getting interesting. Everyone thought Rico and I would get together. I might have to make a wager on Indie and Joseph hooking up first.

JENNA

"*J*oseph, what happened at the morgue today? Do we have rogue vampires? Or do you think they just took advantage of the coming hurricane to steal a few women?" I couldn't help it; I was chewing my nails again.

Every time I think I have kicked the habit, something pops up to make me so nervous, I bite my nails until they're practically bleeding.

"I'm not going to sugar-coat it. I believe we have rogues on the loose." Joseph looked to Rico, who was shaking his head.

"I disagree. With only two bodies, I think they took advantage of the storm." What could make Rico think that?

"That doesn't make sense, Rico. Two bodies that we know of were bitten by vamps. Those weren't gator marks, and we all know it." When the storms brought in higher water levels, the authorities always found bodies.

"Wait, does this mean all of those people who have been discovered after a big storm were murdered by blood-suckers? Even in other states, when they said it was animal bites?" Indie slouched down in her seat and put her plate of Chinese food on the table in front of her.

"I think I lost my appetite." Sam's face fell just like the rest of us.

"Not all reports of death by animals are vamps. Don't worry, the gators and other animals in the swamps still kill humans." Rico sure had a way to cheer us up, not!

"Then please, explain why you think these latest bodies were just vamps taking advantage." Normally I would defer to Rico's judgement in this type of situation. However, I think Joseph may be on to something more.

"Because, there were only two bodies. If we have rogues in the area, there will be many more bodies." Rico pursed his lips and continued to look at Joseph. There was more going on than what Rico was telling us. I just knew it.

"What about all of the missing girls? Is it possible they're dead and their bodies will show up soon?" As much as I hated this idea it was very plausible.

"No. Since the girls have disappeared over the past few weeks, I believe some are doing what their notes said. Others probably were recruited by the vamps. You heard what the University said, this is normal behavior for freshmen." Rico made a good argument, but I didn't agree.

"So, what? These vamps get a free pass since they couldn't pass up a free buffet?" I was not going to accept this. No matter what the reason, they broke their own laws.

"No, it means we get to go hunting." Rico's eyes darkened, and a scary smile crept up his lips.

"How are you going to find the vamps responsible? If they are part of the local coven, then the queen won't be giving them up. We already know she protects her own. Well, until you have actual hard proof. How do you get it?" Kat questioned.

"With good old-fashioned investigative work. The coven will protect their own, but once word gets out we're investigating, certain vamps will go into hiding. Those are the ones we will find. If we're lucky, we might even find a few acolytes who will have a hard time keeping their mouths shut." Rico was really good at his job. I just hoped he could find the ones responsible.

"What does this mean for us? Is there any way we can help? If we can find acolytes, maybe I can help somehow? Or Indie can use her voodoo skills to trick them?" Helping to figure this out was something I needed to do. I don't know why, maybe because of Derek? Either way, I needed to help.

"It means you and your sisters will stick to the Quarter and help clean up. Operate your store and continue your training. If you promise to spend at least two hours a day on cleanup duty or helping your neighbors with their stores, then the pack and I will focus on teaching you more defensive maneuvers and sparring." I couldn't believe Rico was actually going to spend less time with us.

It wasn't a bad thing, but this was weird. I really expected him to hover over me for the next month, at least. He's hiding something.

"Rico, we always help with clean up after a hurricane. That's a given. However, I need to help these girls. One of them was my customer. I feel drawn to this case in a way I haven't since Acadia went missing. You know what happened then, so you better include me." I stood up and crossed my arms over my chest.

Kat, Sam, and Indie all joined me. The four of us stared Rico and Joseph down.

"Dude, if Jenna wants to help find the guys who killed her customer, then we're all helping too. We aren't training our butts off just to sit around and stay safe. Now that we

know the truth, it's up to us to help protect the innocent."
Kat could be difficult when she set her mind to something.
I'm just glad she's backing me up and not Rico.

"Kat, it's too dangerous. Maybe in another year, or two,
you all will be far enough along in your training to help.
Right now, you'll just get into more trouble. Or worse." Rico
could be a real jerk.

Six months of blood, sweat, and tears had turned us into
fighters. Sure, we didn't have special powers, but we could
fight. I am proof of it.

"Joseph, tell Rico we can help. With the protection
charms you're getting us, we should be able to do more. Can
we use other spells? I know we aren't witches, but you sometimes use spells created by them, don't you?" Indie looked
pleadingly into Joseph's eyes.

"Indie, I want you to be safe. I don't want you or your
sisters out there fighting vampires. It's too dangerous. Even I
don't go out alone to fight them, and I grew up training for
this." Joseph rubbed his hands along Indie's arms.

He did seem to care for her and for us.

"How about this? We start out patrolling with several in
your pack. It will help us learn more and, also provide
protection, while we are out working to locate either more
of the missing girls, or the vamps who need to die." This was
a great idea! I don't know why I didn't think of it sooner.

"Hmm. You're going to go out whether I work with you
or not, aren't you?" Rico rubbed his face with both of his
hands. "It might work. As long as you promise to stick to the
group I assign you to."

"Thanks! You won't regret it!" I practically jumped with
my excitement.

This was my chance to actually do something good,
while still having some protection.

"You have to wait until Joseph can get you all protection charms. Once you have them, never take them off. Shower with them, workout with them, swim with them. If it looks like the device they are attached to is wearing out, let Joseph know before you lose the actual charm." Rico mumbled under his breath. I couldn't understand him, but I bet he was regretting this already.

"Rico, you won't regret this. Just like last time, we would have gone out on our own if we had any leads. So working with us is actually keeping us safe. Plus, I bet we can get acolytes to talk to us better than you can." This was one challenge I intended to win.

"Jenna, you haven't encountered an acolyte yet. I think you'll change your mind when you do. They are more like members of a cult than anything else. You can't reason with them." I wondered how many times Rico had encountered acolytes.

"Most of the time it takes torture or months of counseling to get them to see the truth. By then, their information is usually outdated. So torture is the most expedient way to gain intel. Can you torture a girl your age?" Rico had a point.

Torture was not something I ever wanted to deal with. Well, I could probably torture a vampire if he had info about a loved one, but a girl? No, I couldn't do it.

How much practice did Rico and his pack have with torturing?

"Alright, but if there is a chance I can reason with one, I want to try that before you torture them." These girls may have chosen to serve vampires, but I doubt they understood what they were getting into when they volunteered to be blood bags.

"Fine, if you can reason with one, go for it." Rico sighed and sat back down on the couch.

"Just do me one favor?" Rico asked.

"What?" I almost said, 'anything,' but I don't trust him right now.

"Don't tell the next vampire you'll jump his bones?"

I couldn't help it; I busted up laughing, and all three of my sisters as well as Joseph joined me.

"I promise to never jump the bones of a vampire, unless it's in a killing sort of way. How's that?" He had to know I would never, ever, in a million years want a vampire touching me.

"*H*elp! Someone help me!" I heard a woman screaming outside of the shop.

I ran outside to see what was going on. It was early morning and most stores and restaurants hadn't opened yet. I was inside setting up some of the voodoo dolls we had made over the past few nights.

"Hey, what's wrong?" After I looked around, I couldn't see a reason for the yelling. There wasn't anyone else on the street yet.

"Oh! Thank God! Please, you gotta help me!" A terrified young woman, who looked to have just barely made it through the hurricane, followed me into the shop.

She turned her wide eyes out the window and locked my door. Then she went and hid behind the counter. "Quick, before he sees you. Get over here and hide!"

I looked out the window but didn't see anyone. As I turned around I did catch a shadow turning the corner. Without even thinking, I ducked down and shuffled over to where the girl was.

She had to be younger than me, maybe eighteen, and

she had a rat's nest on what looked to have once been long auburn hair. Her bugged-out eyes told me she was either strung out...or in total fear of her life.

"What happened?" Where did I begin? Should I call the cops or Rico?

"I ran away from them. They sent one of their goons after me. You're the only person who has opened their door for me! Thank you! Do you have any weapons?" She huddled underneath the counter which held my cash register. My cell phone was sitting up on top of the counter.

"Who did you run away from?" I tried to move closer to her, but she pulled her knees up in front of her face and shivered. "Are you cold? Do you want some coffee or tea?"

I crawled to the back room and turned on the tea kettle. Without knowing what the shadow was, I didn't want to draw attention to me. Especially since there weren't any people out on the street yet. The sun had barely risen. Most shops were still closed while they continued their repairs from the hurricane.

It seemed most shop owners weren't as prepared as usual. They listened to Sasha and believed it would only be a tropical storm, until she changed her mind at the last minute. Hurricane Gerttie passed us by, barely. However, it left a ton of damage in its wake.

Those who didn't get their storm shutters up returned to major damage. Others, like us, got our storm shutters up and the ground cleared. Mold was the worst thing we were dealing with.

"Here, have some tea. This should help warm you up. I'm going to call a friend who can help you. Should I also call the police?" Until I knew what we were dealing with, I wasn't sure I should involve the cops.

"Don't call the cops! They can't help. No one can. This is

a voodoo shop, right? Do you have any spells to keep vampires away?" The girl sipped her tea and it hit me who she was.

"You're one of the missing storm girls, aren't you? Did you just say vampires?" I crawled over to the counter and peeked above to grab my phone and see if anyone was outside the shop.

A huge guy walked by and looked inside right when I peeked over the counter. Our eyes met, and he looked to be growling.

"Open up! I know she's in there. Turn her over to me, and I'll leave you alone." The burly guy outside the door yelled before he began pounding on the door.

Ignoring him, I dialed Rico.

"Jenna, it's a bit early isn't it?" His hoarse voice answered.

"Rico! We're in trouble. Some guy is outside my shop trying to break in. I rescued one of the missing girls. This guy was following her. Can you send anyone to help?"

"What? It's light out, right? Then it can't be a vampire. It must be one of their acolytes they use for daylight muscle. Do you still have a gun?"

"Yes! We put it in the store room after the last time we needed it. Do I shoot him? If he's human, I don't want to kill him." That was the last thing I wanted, but I also didn't want him getting inside and hurting me or this poor girl.

"Don't worry about it. Be sure to protect yourself. Remember, he willingly works for the vamps. He's most likely next on the list to be turned, which is why they sent him after the girl. If she really was taken by vamps." I could hear Rico getting ready in the background.

"She told me she ran away from vampires."

Rico put his hand over the phone and called out to Damien, "Do we have anyone in town? Jenna's at the shop and in trouble. We need to send someone there right away. If not, then a cop you trust."

"Jenna, is he still outside?" Rico calmly asked me.

"Yes, but he's pounding on the door. He's gonna break it any minute now." I ran to the store room and pulled the locked case down from the top of the rack. It held a handgun Kat had been keeping in our apartment upstairs.

"I've got the gun."

"Where's the girl?" Rico was running. I could hear the strain in his voice.

"She's hiding under the counter and kinda freaking out. This is what you trained me for. I can do this." I had to psych myself up for fighting a human.

At this point, I realized it would have been easier to fight a vampire than a human. I didn't want to hurt a human but had no trouble killing a vamp if given the chance.

"Rico, I'm going to put the phone on the counter and put you on speaker so you can hear it all. Then I'm pointing the gun at the front door. The second he comes through, I'm shooting. Can I do that?" I wasn't sure what the laws were concerning shooting someone who broke into my store.

Since it technically was part of my house, I might be within the bounds of the law. Or I might not be. I wasn't going to prison for this cretan who worshiped blood-suckers.

"Open up! I'm not going to give you another chance! She belongs to my masters, and they want her back!" The guy sure did have a set of lungs on him.

If any of the shopkeepers on this street were in, they would most certainly be calling the cops. Fine, let them come and deal with the dangerous guy. In fact, it would be better if cops showed up instead of me having to shoot him.

"Rico, he's making a lot of noise. Even though it's really

early, someone is bound to hear him and call the cops. Do you think they can deal with this guy?" I had already put the phone on speaker.

"It depends on who shows up. I'll be there as fast as I can. Damien is looking to see if anyone is still in town. If not, he's going to call a cop buddy of his who has an idea of what's really going on. Hopefully, someone will arrive before he breaks in."

Kat, Indie, and Sam all ran down the stairs. Each carrying a different weapon.

"What's going on? Who's that idiot outside trying to break in?" Kat held the other gun in her hand ready to shoot.

Indie and Sam both held baseball bats. Little known trick is to keep those around. Since they're sporting equipment, you can't really get into trouble for having a deadly weapon. Who doesn't have a bat, ball, and gloves in their house these days? It is the great American pastime, after all.

"Oh, good. That guy out there might be an acolyte. Look who showed up on our door claiming to have run away from vampires?" I pointed to the girl covering her neck and was curled up into the tightest ball she could get into, right under our counter.

Poor thing was rocking back and forth and shaking her head.

"No, No, NO! Don't let him take me! Those vampires wanted to do awful things to me. Please don't! Not again!" The girl was hysterical and sobbing between the words.

Sam kneeled down next to her. "Don't worry, we're going to protect you. Those vampires will never hurt you again."

I wanted to look at my sister as she tried to calm the poor girl, but I had to keep my eyes on the door. The brute had already cracked the window in our door. It was made of glass and steel, mostly glass. Once he got those cracks bigger, he was going to get through.

"Great! Our shop survived a hurricane, but it's going to be torn apart by some dipstick who serves agents of the devil! Just our luck." Indie was mad. She tightened her grip on the bat and stood off to the side of the counter.

It only took a couple more hits by the demon lover with the gargantuan arms. I don't know how someone gets that size. He had to be six feet, five inches tall with forearms the size of my thighs, if not bigger! He has some serious power in him.

I began to rethink my idea of not shooting. If I didn't shoot, he would probably kill me, or worse!

There were four women all holding weapons, two of which were guns, but that didn't stop him from breaking the door and running in.

He was like a mad-man on PCP or something. I heard a shot ring out, it wasn't from me. Kat must have already shot him.

He wasn't falling. The monster kept moving like getting shot in the shoulder was nothing. I saw the blood on his right shoulder, where I imagined Kat's bullet hit him. She shot again and hit him in the chest.

The giant kept coming.

I shot, without even realizing it. The only reason I knew I shot off a bullet was because of the recoil on the gun. It wasn't much but enough to let me know I had actually shot a human being.

My bullet got him in his gut.

I kept shooting. I'm not sure when Kat stopped, but I didn't stop until the guy was no longer moving on the ground. It could have also been because I was out of bullets.

My gun only held six. Somewhere in the back of my mind, I registered the fact I used them all up.

"Indie, give me your bat. Go upstairs and get more ammo. I keep it in my desk drawer. This monster should be dead, but I've never seen someone take so many bullets and keep going. I want more ammo just to be on the safe side." Kat took the bat from Indie, before she ran upstairs.

The girl was still under the counter and sobbing.

"Hey, he's not going to hurt you. Do you know if there were any more guys chasing you?" Probably something I should have asked sooner.

"I...I don't think so. There weren't very many men in the group. I don't know. I can't be sure." She stopped rocking and looked up at me with her tear-stained face.

When she moved her hand to wipe the tears, I saw the marks. She had been in the clutches of vampires alright. I stooped down and moved her head back and forth slowly. The neck of her shirt had been ripped, and I counted at least four sets of bite marks on her neck.

"OH.MY.GOODNESS! How in the world did you survive this?" If she had that many feeding off her over the past few days, how was she still alive?

She shook her head and began crying again. I couldn't blame her.

In the distance I could hear the sounds of sirens. I really hoped the cops would understand.

"Luke! Thank goodness! Were you close by?" Sam ran over and gave him a hug as he tried to make his way into our store.

"What happened? How did he break the glass on your door? That was an industrial strength door." Luke examined the door frame before walking over and kicking the body.

"Is he dead?" Indie asked when she walked through the store room. She had a box of ammo in her hand.

Luke looked up at all of us. "You might want to put the ammo away out of sight. Also, I would put those guns on the other counter before the cops get here. Did you fire them both?"

I nodded and wished I hadn't needed to shoot the gun in my hand. However, I was very grateful we had both guns and were able to use them today. If the monster lying on my floor had made it to us, I have no doubt I would be the next thing up on the vampire's menu.

Two cops walked into my store with their guns drawn.

"We heard reports of guns fired. Where are the guns?" The cop on the left asked.

I pointed to the counter where Kat put both of our guns.

The other cop called in using the radio attached to his shoulder. He used numbers and code words that went right over my head.

"Jenna! Thank the good Lord you're alright!" Rico ran right to me and hugged me tightly.

I'll be honest, tears were streaming down my face, and I didn't want him to let me go.

"Rico, he kept coming. He wouldn't stop." I blabbered in his chest.

"Shhh, be quiet. Don't say anything until Damien arrives," Rico whispered in my ear.

"Excuse me, but what happened here?" One of the cops asked Kat.

Before she could answer, the girl who had been hiding under my counter stood up. "They saved my life."

"Hey, aren't you Lisa or Gina? One of the missing college girls?" Cop number two slowly moved closer to her.

"Lisa, and yes. I was abducted when I tried to evacuate before the hurricane. These girls saved my life from that... that thing on the ground!" She pointed a shaky finger at the dead guy.

I could hear more sirens coming to my shop. Damien walked through the broken door with another cop on his heels.

This one must have been a detective. He was in plain clothes but wore a badge on a rope around his neck, like in the movies.

"Officers, I'll take it from here. Please make sure to prepare a fifteen foot perimeter of the shop. Keep out anyone who doesn't belong." The new guy had a look on his face which told me he was not to be messed with. His eyes were narrow, and his lips were pursed.

"Rico, it's good to see you again. I see you and your friends have gotten me into another unexplainable mess. At this rate, I'll never make Captain." The detective walked around the body after he put on those blue booties and matching blue latex gloves.

"I'm Detective Adams. Who wants to tell me what happened here?" He looked right at me when he asked.

"I was working in the shop early, trying to re-stock the shelves before we opened. I heard someone screaming for help outside, so I opened the door and that poor woman ran inside." I continued to tell my story until the paramedics arrived.

"Detective, this woman needs medical treatment. We're

taking her to the hospital." The paramedic had his arm around Lisa and began to walk her outside.

"Wait, what's your name?" The detective stood in their path.

"Lisa. Lisa Greenwood." She kept her gaze on me while she stood in front of the detective.

"You're one of the missing girls. Were there others where you were?" The detective had taken out his pen and pad.

"Yes, I think there were three more girls still alive." When Lisa dropped that bombshell, the entire room went silent.

13

JENNA

"*O*h!" I gasped into Rico's chest.

"Detective, you can't let her leave yet. We need to know where the girls are located. If they are still alive, we have to find them. Now." Rico let me go and walked over to Lisa.

"I can grab my kit and start to treat her here, if you want to question her. Is there a cot or a sofa we can sit on?" The paramedic's eyes were still bugged out as he looked Lisa up and down.

"Yes, we have a back room here in the store or our apartment above. Feel free to use whatever space you need. Please, let me know if we can help. We all have some first aid training." Kat motioned to the back room where we had a very small break room that housed a sofa and a few chairs.

"You might want to go upstairs. It will be quieter and more comfortable there." Rico led the girl and the detective to the back stairs.

"Damien, what do we do now?" I watched as the CSI guys took photos of my broken shop.

I wondered how many of the voodoo dolls would have to

be trashed. Stupid, I know, but my mind was having trouble processing what was going on. A human was dead, and a missing girl had just turned up in my shop claiming there were more girls still alive.

This meant there had to be something really big going down with the local vamps. I hoped this wasn't the beginning of the impending war. A few months ago we learned there were some vampires working with witches on a plan to overthrow the vampire queen. While she wasn't going to win any popularity contests, she kept her vampires in line, mostly.

"Does this mean war?" This was so over my head.

"I don't know yet. My guess is yes. I just hope there is something else going on here, like some feral vamps who were never claimed and taught how to feed. It's the best we can hope for at this time. Otherwise, I don't want to even think what might be coming." Damien ran a hand through his hair and put his other hand on my lower back.

"Come on, we should go upstairs and let the crime scene investigators do their job. Besides, Detective Adams will need a statement from each of you as well. Don't be surprised if more cops and detectives show up." Damien led us up to our own apartment.

"Word of caution, if anyone other than Adams wants to question you, don't say anything without me present. I'm your lawyer. Got it?" Damien looked me in the eye.

"I didn't know you were an attorney. How long have you practiced law?" Indie stopped on the steps and turned around to ask.

"I only represent our pack, which includes all four of you girls. If you are ever arrested, just tell them I'm your attorney, and you won't say a word until I arrive. Got it?" Damien was one interesting guy.

I bet he had a lot of stories to tell. One of these days I had to sit him down and ask him to share.

*

*I*t was after eight at night when we returned from the local police department.

"I can't believe they made us go down to the station and fill out forms and be recorded." I blew my bangs out of my eyes and plopped down on the sofa.

"I'm starving. Do we have anything to eat? I don't feel like cooking. Maybe some Chinese leftovers?" Sam went into the kitchen and opened the fridge door.

"Not enough leftovers for all of us. Can we send Rico or one of his guys to Uncle Wong's?" Sam pulled out a bottle of water for each of us.

"Sure, I'll call him and see who's patrolling." I pulled out my phone and dialed Rico.

"Hey, I just dropped you off. Is everything alright? Or do you just miss me already?" I really didn't feel like our usual banter.

"Actually, we're all starving, and there's nothing quick to eat in the house. Can you send someone to Uncle Wong's for us? I'll call in an order."

"Really? You aren't going to go and get it yourself? I'm surprised, Jenna."

"I would, normally. Tonight, I'm too tired to deal with anything. I just want food and my bed. That's all. Maybe not even in that order." A headache was starting to develop.

When I was really stressed, I would get tension headaches. Today totally qualified for a mega stressful day. It's not every day you kill a man and get hauled into the police station to give your testimony.

"Sorry, I should have thought of that. I am glad you called me first. I'll go by and pick it up. Just call Jimmie with your order." Rico hung up before I could even ask him if he wanted anything.

After we all had full tummies, my sisters drew numbers to see who would get a long, hot bath tonight. We all loved our baths, but we only had one tub.

"Yeah! I think." Indie drew the short straw, meaning she got the first bath.

"I know, part of me just wants to go to bed and deal with a shower in the morning." Kat dragged herself up and headed to the shower first.

Since Rico was still here, I agreed to shower last, if I even lasted that long. But, it meant I could take the first bath tomorrow.

"How long before we can open up the store again?" Rico had dealt with the cops, when we were at the station, while I was giving my testimony over and over with the detectives.

"CSI still isn't done with your store. They did put up some plywood to cover your open door, but I think they might want another day to investigate. You and your sisters will have to stay away until they give you the all clear."

"Once they do, let me know. I'll bring over a few guys to help clean up. You might want to get a new door ordered tomorrow. I'm not sure how long it will take to get it." Rico had become like family to us.

He always looked out for me and my sisters.

"Thanks, Rico. I really appreciate everything you and your pack does for us. I doubt we thank you enough. Just know we are here if you need anything." I would never be able to repay his kindness.

"How about a hug?" Rico moved next to me on the couch and pulled me up next to him.

He felt so good and warm. This was what it felt like to be truly protected and cared for. Why couldn't I let my heart open up to him?

Rico leaned over and kissed the top of my head.

I sighed and relaxed against him.

14

JENNA

The next thing I knew, it was morning, and I was lying on the couch wrapped in Rico's arms.

"Good morning, sunshine." Rico whispered in my ear. He was behind me with his back against the rear of the sofa, and my rear was up against his body. It was kinda hot. Not in the I need a cold drink kinda way, it was more in the I need a cold shower kinda way.

Wolves must be really warm-blooded. We didn't have a blanket on us, but I was warm and toasty. Not to mention I slept better than I could remember since being dragged into the seedy underbelly of New Orleans and magic

"Mmm. Good morning. Did I fall asleep in your arms last night? You could have left me here on the couch, or woken me up. I doubt it was very comfortable for you." I rubbed the sleep from my eyes.

"It was more than comfortable." He nuzzled my neck, and I grabbed his arm which was wrapped around my waist.

"I think I need to get up and hop in the shower. Your pack is probably wondering where you are right now." My breathing was shallow, and I knew in that moment I was about to make a big mistake if I didn't get moving.

My entire body screamed for me to turn around and kiss him.

I jumped up and moved across the room from him before my instincts, or his, took control. I knew he wanted me. The feeling was mutual. However, this was not going to happen.

I always screwed things up or chose a guy who screwed things up. None of my past relationships ended on a good note. Not one. If I started something with Rico and it ended badly, like I expected, I would be losing out on the best friend I ever had.

There was no way I was going to take that chance.

"Jenna, what's wrong? I know you feel the way I do. Why do you keep pulling back?" Wow, Rico wasn't playing any games this morning.

Was he always so direct first thing in the morning? Or just when he woke up with me in his arms?

"Rico, of course I have feelings for you." I ran a hand through my hair and tried to figure out how to put my thoughts into words.

"I...You...We have gone through so much. Over the past seven or eight months I have come to depend on you so much. Other than my sisters, you're the closest friend I have. I couldn't stand to lose your friendship." My heart was breaking, and my mind was screaming at me to shut up and kiss the guy.

"Jenna, no matter what..." Rico was interrupted when Indie and Sam walked into the room half awake.

"Hey, did you two stay up all night?" Indie's forehead scrunched up when she noticed Rico on the couch.

"We fell asleep out here. Sorry if we woke you. It's early,

and we can't get in the shop, so you might as well go back to sleep." I noticed both of my sisters were still in their pajamas. Hopefully they would take my advice.

"Nah, we still have a lot of work to do. I imagine a lot of the voodoo dolls, and even some of our potions and charms, were destroyed. Indie and I decided to get up early and get a head start on making up more inventory." Sam walked into the kitchen.

"You want coffee?" Sam called over her shoulder while she set up the machine.

"Yes! Please." I needed caffeine in a bad way.

"I'll go and see if any of the local cafés are open. Who's up for a beignet?" Rico asked when he stood up.

All three of us raised our hands. Kat was still in her room.

"Might as well get one for Kat, too. I'm sure she'll want one." I looked at Rico's back when he made for the front door.

The second the door closed behind Rico, both of my sisters boxed me in against the wall. "Spill. What happened last night?" Sam's eyes sparkled with her mirth.

"Nothing happened, I just fell asleep, and for some reason, he stayed." I looked between my two sisters who both wore smirks.

"Uh, huh. And I have a bridge to sell you." Sam crossed her arms over her chest.

"You might as well tell us. We aren't letting you go until you do." Indie winked.

"Ugh! Please! If something happened I would totally tell you. No, it's not what you think. I'm sure he stayed here to keep an eye on us all overnight." I pushed against my sisters and went to the kitchen for some fresh coffee.

"What do you mean?" Indie asked as she trailed me into our tiny kitchen.

"Think about it. He tried to keep us from listening in on what Lisa had to say whenever she talked about where she had been." I reached into the fridge for creamer.

"True. He knows us well enough now to suspect we would have gone after those other girls last night, if we could have. I think we have learned enough to know better than to go looking for a vampire's nest at night, though. I was going to suggest going out today and looking." Sam pulled down another mug from cupboard.

I couldn't help but laugh. We were totally on the same frequency. Looking for the missing girls in the daylight is a much better idea. One I was thinking about as well.

"I think Rico stayed over to make sure none of us left last night. Although, if he really thought about it, we were too tired and worn out to go anywhere. So what do you think he's up to today?" Indie leaned against the stove and watched while I made my cup of coffee.

Sipping my coffee, I thought about what she asked.

"He ran out of here pretty quickly. I bet he's calling Damien or Joseph to find out if anyone learned anything on patrol last night. I would be willing to bet big money he sent out as many pack members as possible last night to check the usual haunts. See if they could find out where the girls are being kept." Man this was good coffee.

My shoulders relaxed, and I sighed as I realized it was exactly what the doctor ordered for my headache.

"Ok, so he probably has an idea of the area those missing girls are in. What do we do now?" Sam asked before sipping her coffee.

Indie moved me aside so she could make herself a cup.

"I think we focus on creating more inventory today and let the experts look for the girls."

"What? You don't want to help find them?" I couldn't believe what Indie was saying. She's normally the type to run straight into trouble, without even thinking.

"I know. That's not normally me. However, think about it. We still have a lot of training to do. These vampires aren't playing by the rules. There is something much bigger going on here than we realize. If this has to do with the pending war, or coup, or whatever it is those vamps and witches are up to, do you really think we have a chance?" Okay, Indie had a point.

"Hmm, you might be on to something there. I guess if the pack knows where to look, we should let them handle it. For now. There is a lot of work to do here and as we have said many times, we don't have magic." I drained the rest of my coffee and went back for another cup.

"For now. I'm hoping Joseph can get us some real charms and maybe even a few spells we can use for protection, just in case. I'm talking real magic, not voodoo stuff. Although, I wouldn't mind making a few vampire voodoo dolls. Do you think those would sell well?" Indie smiled over the brim of her coffee mug.

"Only you would think about making vampire voodoo dolls." We all jumped when Kat joined us in the kitchen. Sometimes she could be very sneaky.

"What, you don't think with all of the stuff going on around here that residents wouldn't want a vamp voodoo doll? I, for one, think it's genius." Sam walked into the living room with her cup of coffee.

"Alright, let's make a few and see how they sell. It can't hurt. Just don't go spreading any rumors that vampires are real. That's all we need, a city full of stressed out people trying to clean up from the hurricane and freaking out over real vampires." Kat grabbed her own cup of coffee.

"We could say they are more metaphorical creatures. You know, like an ex who can't stop trying to mooch off you. He's a vampire in a way." Indie sure knew her voodoo dolls.

"That's brilliant! I bet we make a fortune on them!" Sam ran to the store room to grab supplies, and we all set up our work areas in the living room to make the new Vampire Voodoo Dolls the rest of the day.

*R*ico knocked on the door about an hour later. To be honest, I sorta forgot he left to get us pastries.

"Hey, where'd ya go? I thought you were bringing us back some breakfast?" I answered the door.

"I received a call from Damien, and then had to find a place which was open and serving. Most stores haven't re-opened fully yet. Your favorite coffee shop around the corner is only doing coffee, tea, water and some sandwiches. Basically easy stuff most people are going to need while cleaning up the city." Rico walked in with two bags and a coffee carrier.

"Is that my favorite coffee in your hands? Or just regular drip coffee?" I smelled the eye-opening aroma coffee.

"It's your favorite roast. I thought I would bring a bunch over here and tell my pack to come by for some coffee when they are in the area, if that's alright? I also have some of the pre-packaged sandwiches." He set his load on the kitchen counter.

"Sure, your pack is always welcome here. We should probably fix up some more stuff, like tea and cookies. I have a feeling the city will sell out quickly today if there are a lot of clean-up crews around." Kat looked inside of the bags and began pulling sandwiches out and putting them into the fridge.

"If you don't mind, I asked Joseph to come over here after he sees his witch buddy. Getting out to our place takes time right now. The city is still cleaning up the highway. We can drive here and back, but it is a waste of time. Would you mind if we held meetings here until we find those missing girls? It could really help save time if we just come into the city and stay here all day." I couldn't believe Rico was actually going to conduct meetings in front of us.

Would he share this information with us if we offered up our place? Or was this just another way for him to keep an eye on us? Probably the latter.

"Sure, feel free to hang out here. Just be warned, if anyone sits around for too long, Indie will probably put them to work on vampire voodoo dolls." Sam laughed.

"What? Vampire voodoo dolls? Is that a thing?" Rico scratched his chin.

"Yup. We're making it a new craze. I expect with all of the breakups after a hurricane we will see record sales over the coming month. Plus, a lot of the women, and even some men, will think their ex's are more like vampires, trying to suck the life out of them." Sam held up a doll she had just began working on.

"What do you think? Good vampire? Or bad?" Sam twisted the doll around for all of us to see.

"Maybe add a couple drops of red dye to look like blood on the mouth? I think you might have something here. Indie, watch out, or Sam is going to pass up your mad voodoo skills with her own!" I loved teasing them when it came to this sort of stuff.

We were finally starting to get our groove back, which

was nice. Since the night before the hurricane, I hadn't felt normal. So much has happened over the past week, who could feel normal? This however, was normal and nice.

Indie ran to her room and grabbed a doll that looked like me! How dare she!

"Jenna, watch out. You don't want more headaches, do you?" Indie took a pin and poked it into my doll's head. She always did this when she was being a stinker.

"Indie, I learned to keep my own doll." I ran to my room and grabbed my own Indie doll and set of pins I kept just for her.

"How does your stomach feel?" I poked a pin into the Indie doll's stomach.

"Knock it off, we don't have time for goofing off. Save it for later, after we have restocked the store." Kat shook her head and grabbed a pastry from Rico's bags.

"Ugh, prepackaged croissants? Really, Rico. Why even waste the money?" Kat took one bite and threw it away.

"Kat, my guys like those things. Plus, they are easy to carry around and pull out when you need a snack on patrol. Just leave them alone if you don't like packaged pastries." Rico took a few out of one of the bags and set them aside on the counter.

It actually wasn't a bad idea, prepacked food could be handy. Although, it did usually taste like cardboard or paper.

I think we were all spoiled by Indie. She was into whole foods and rarely allowed microwave meals in our house. Everything had to be freshly made. One of the reasons we ordered from Uncle Wong's so much is because he was a believer in fresh and organic foods. His prices were a bit higher, but his food was much tastier for it.

"Rico, do you have any news for us regarding the

charms?" I was getting antsy sitting around waiting to be able to join them on patrols.

Rico said we had to wait for the magical charms before we could join him and his pack. I was itching to get out there and kick some serious vampire butt.

"I'll text Joseph and see what he says." Rico pulled his phone out of his back pocket and began texting.

15

RICO

"Just got a text from Joseph, he's down the street. He has a surprise for you, Indie." I pocketed my cell phone and got back to helping the girls with the eyes on their voodoo dolls.

I had been wrangled into sewing on various eyes. Mostly, it was just buttons. However, some of the eyes were a bit different. They were made out of material with an eyeball painted on them. Those were the creepiest of all of the voodoo dolls.

It's no wonder so many people swore by their dolls. I would imagine the power of the mind could make you think some really weird stuff was going on with these things.

"Oh! I love surprises! I hope it's magical in nature!" Indie was the reason I was helping with the voodoo dolls. How could you say no to someone with so much vivacity?

Indie was sitting at the sewing machine. They had dolls made from fabric and stuffed with some white fluff. They also had dolls made from dried up corn husks. They were all very different, but some seemed to have the same, eerie faces painted on them. No clue how they managed to do it.

"I think you might be pleasantly surprised." This was one secret I was going to hold on to. Joseph had worked miracles if what he said was true.

Not thirty minutes later, Joseph was knocking on the door, and I was sick and tired of sewing on creepy eyeballs.

"It's about time! What took you so long?" I complained when I opened up the door.

"Sorry, boss. I had to stop and see if I could get some beignets. The shop around the corner had a long line. By the time I got to the front, they were all out." Joseph walked into the room carrying a leather satchel.

It wasn't familiar to me. He rarely carried a bag. When he did it was more of canvas messenger bag. This leather satchel looked to be stuffed with something.

"What do you have in your goody bag?" Indie asked when she greeted Joseph with a hug.

Were these two also stuck in the same rut as Jenna and I? Would they ever get past the 'just friends' wall?

"I have some much anticipated treats! Along with some extra special items I think you might be very interested in." Joseph closed the door before coming inside and joining the rest of us at the table.

He opened up the cover of his bag and pulled out a smaller pouch. It was a cloth bag with magical symbols on it. The bag itself was blue and green, but there were symbols sewn into the fabric. Some looked similar to the basic alchemy symbols, using the sun and moon.

Joseph opened up the zipper of the smaller bag and put his hand inside. He pulled out a rather nice bracelet. It was made of leather and a few purple beads. The top part of the bracelet held a charm which resembled the inside of an oyster.

"This is a protection charm for you, Jenna." She put her hand out to Joseph and ooh'd and awe'd over the pretty trinket.

"It's purple! How perfect for me. Is this like what Rico wears around his neck?"

I did not wear anything purple, or pretty, around my neck.

Joseph chuckled. "Yes, it holds the protection charm. You have to wear it at all times. Never take it off, not even to shower. The leather straps will last a long time, even in water. If you begin to see fraying, let me know, and I'll get you a new one. It should last a couple of years."

"This charm has an added bonus. Vamps are magical creatures. The charm bracelet protects against fangs. It's more of a prototype. My friend said these are the first he has created. Don't rely on them to repel blood suckers. These bracelets will repel magic up to a certain level as well as fangs. Anything more than those two and you need the other charms and spells I have for you."

I wondered why the witch's council allowed this. Surely Joseph's contact would not have created all of these spells without approval. Why did he make so many for Jenna and her sisters?

"Here, Kat." Joseph pulled another bracelet out, it was identical to Jenna's, except it held blue beads.

"I was able to get the witch to make your charms to match your hair." My alchemist pulled out the remaining two bracelets and handed them to Indie and Sam.

Joseph helped Indie put hers on before helping anyone else.

"Thank you! What else did you bring? Anything else fun?" Indie wiggled her brows, after she admired the jewelry on her wrist.

"In fact, I do have something fun for each of you." Joseph put his bag on the ground after pulling out another zippered cloth bag. This one was much bigger and looked to be what held the items making the bulge in his satchel.

"I have various defensive and offensive spells you can use." I was shocked Joseph's witch contact gave him so many spells for the girls to use.

He couldn't have told his friend who was getting these. I couldn't even get his friend to make me spells, other than the amulet around my neck.

"Here, these are all various defensive spells tied to necklaces and bracelets. They are one time use only. You can wear them as jewelry, but remember, once you activate them, they are no longer any good." Joseph pulled out four necklaces which matched the girl's bracelets.

"These are the ones you want to always wear in case of an emergency. When you activate this it shrouds you in a protective barrier. Only a witch more powerful than my friend can break it down. The downside is the shield only lasts about two minutes. So don't use it unless your life is in imminent danger." Joseph put one around Indie's neck and handed the rest out to the girls.

"Well, at least our jewelry will match." Jenna put the charm around her neck.

"So, it's like a one-time-use disposable camera? You get a fun benefit but can only use it once? The package is still there, you just can't take any more pictures? Or in our case, use the spell a second time?" Kat examined her necklace.

She seemed to have a better understanding of real magic than the rest of the girls. I wondered how much Ivan had told her since they met.

"Exactly. Now, check out these stones. They are color

coded so be sure to learn the colors. The most important one is red. If you throw a red stone at someone it will kill them. So don't use them on humans. It's a waste of the stone. Only use them on vampires." Joseph really scored when he met with his contact.

"Joseph, how did you get so many spells from your friend? He's never agreed to give more than a couple to you for your own use. How did you do this?"

"The witches want us to destroy the vampires. I think they will be selling us more spells going forward, or at least, until the threat is neutralized. My friend, Aleric, has been ordered by the witch's council to make sure we have enough low level spells to use against the vamps. He said they didn't tell him exactly what was going on, but they know a war is coming." Joseph was smart to work that friendship all of those years ago.

Now, I wish I would have tried harder to make friends with witches.

Indie walked up to Joseph and stepped up on her tiptoes to kiss his cheek. "Thank you, Joseph. This is going to help out so much! Now we don't have to worry so much."

"We can go to Uncle Wong's whenever we want Chinese!" Jenna smiled when she looked at me.

I couldn't help it, I had to chuckle at everyone's excitement.

"This doesn't mean you have free reign of the night. These spells will help you, but you still have to fight. Most importantly, you still have to use good, common sense and not go anywhere alone. I doubt you would be able to fight off a pack of vampires intent on making you their midnight snack. Even with the magical charms." This is what worried me the most, them thinking they were now invincible.

If I was honest with myself, I think I was more worried Jenna wouldn't need me as much now. Which was just a crazy thought. Her safety was paramount. If having these spells would help to keep her and her sisters safe from the blood-suckers, then I could handle receiving fewer calls of help from her.

"I know, we can't go anywhere alone, and we have to watch where we go after dark. I get it, I do. It's just now we have a bit more freedom, and you can stop worrying about us." Jenna was wrong. I would always worry about her.

"Ladies, just remember, the stones have to touch the body of the intended target. Except the red one. This stone." Joseph held up a sparking red stone for all to see. "This just needs to get close."

"So, close is good enough for horseshoes, hand grenades, and red stones?" Indie really was crazy at times. However, she was accurate.

"The guys should be here shortly. Joseph, can you help me set up some chairs? We need to coordinate our efforts to locate the girls. I want them found by tonight. I don't trust the vamps to keep them alive much longer." I was shocked some of the girls were still alive.

This new information had me reexamining my conclusions about who took them.

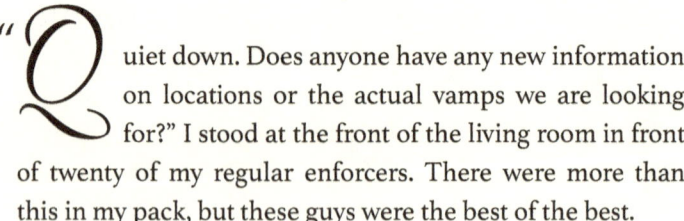

"Quiet down. Does anyone have any new information on locations or the actual vamps we are looking for?" I stood at the front of the living room in front of twenty of my regular enforcers. There were more than this in my pack, but these guys were the best of the best.

Luke stood up. "I think they might be close to the neighborhood we busted up a few months back. Pretty stupid, if you ask me. Last night I saw a few vampires in the street next to where we found Acadia."

"I thought the queen abandoned that neighborhood? Didn't she want to put as much distance between her coven and those vampires who broke the law?" Jose asked.

"Yes, I patrolled those streets not two weeks ago, and the houses were still vacant. Are you saying there are people living in the houses? Or underneath them?" I had even gone through one of the tunnels looking to see if vamps were hiding out there. Dust had started to settle inside the house, and there were enough signs of rats, I assumed the vamps hadn't been back since.

"I saw two vampires and one male acolyte walking down the street. I followed them, and they went inside one of the abandoned houses. They could have just been scavenging, or they could be staying there. I'm not sure. We need to go back and take a closer look." Luke could lead the team checking out the neighborhood.

"Alright, grab a team of ten wolves and be there before the sun sets. I want all of the houses checked out before going underground, preferably during the day." One team down.

"Anyone else have targets?"

Damien stood. "I wanted to check the old factories. You know, the ones we've seen rogue vampires use before."

"Yes, I know the ones." It took every ounce of willpower not to look at Jenna.

Damien was referencing the location Jenna almost died earlier this year when a rogue vamp kidnapped her. Those abandoned warehouses would be a great place to hole up, especially for rogues.

"Damien, you lead a team of at least fifteen. Call back to

the compound and get some more wolves to come in. That place is really large, and I don't want anyone going in alone, understand?" If I could keep at least teams of two together, our guys would have a better chance of survival.

Most of our fighters were men. Although, I did have a few women who were tougher than most of my men. They just chose to protect the compound instead of coming into town for patrols.

Sometimes they wanted to change things up and would join a patrol, but with all of the families we had, our fighting women chose to stay home and protect the pack. While I had great respect for their decision, they might need to join the hunt this time.

"Jose, call ReeAnna and see if she can get a team together to come and patrol the city while we are searching the two target locations. I don't like the idea of having no one in the city to protect the humans, especially right now." With the hurricane damage, not as many tourists have returned yet, so the streets aren't as safe as usual.

"Joseph, will you stay here with the girls? I want to go with Luke and check out the neighborhood. Something bugs me about what he saw. I have a bad feeling about the place." Rubbing my jaw, I sat down and considered what it could all mean.

If vampires are returning to the neighborhood, is the queen condoning these attacks? I would have to pay her a visit, probably tomorrow. I wanted to get more information before speaking with her. She was never very forthright. The more I knew, the more I could get out of her.

"Of course. I can use this time to train them more on the use of the magical charms I brought them." Joseph could always be depended upon.

His alchemy background helped him to understand the

chemical makeup of the spells the witches used. He also had created some flash bangs as well as a few potions of his own to counteract spells. They didn't always work, but more often than not, science could be used against magic, if you knew the ancient alchemy secrets.

16

RICO

"*L*uke, you take lead on this. I'm just here as back-up." I also wanted to check out what's happened since the last time I was here.

The tunnels connected to most of the houses within a few blocks should still be swamped from the hurricane. It seemed very odd the vamps were here at this time.

Surely they had to know we would check this place out whenever there was a vamp problem. Right? Or were they this stupid?

"Sure thing, boss." Luke was a good Lieutenant and would lead this mission well. He just needed a bit more practice, and then he would be great.

"Simon, Roger, Rock, Gustave, and Remy. I want all five of you in wolf form. Sniff out the vamps and their trails. The rest, stay human unless you need to shift in order to fight. We need to keep a few humans in case we come across the girls. I doubt they will be open to us in our shifted state." Luke directed the wolves and men on where to go, and I followed my nose.

When I was here last, I fought beneath one of the houses

two streets away. I intended to check it out, along with the tunnels underneath. First, I needed to ensure all of my men were on target and didn't need me.

"Luke, I think you know where I want to go. Do you have this all under control? Or do you need me to do anything first?" My nose had picked up on a scent.

In human form we had excellent senses, but in wolf form it went to a whole new level. If my human nose smelled vamps, there must be some very close by.

"Rico, I think I have it under control. Just be safe. I'm sure you smell them. I have no idea why they are here, or where they are, but there are vampires close by." Luke nodded, and I stalked off toward my target.

"You too, Luke."

With my ears on alert, and my nose smelling the stench of death, I took off to find the house where Acadia almost died.

Quietly, I crept along in the shadows. I kept my eyes and ears alert for any sounds or smells which didn't belong. When I was about halfway to the street, I heard a crunch. Someone had stepped on a dry leaf or paper. The sound came from around the house I was approaching.

With my back up against the house, I slowly inched my way to the edge of the wall and peered around the corner. In the yard was a human male. He didn't look familiar, and he carried a gun.

As far as I knew, the locals near this neighborhood avoided it like the plague. While I doubted they knew the truth, they suspected something was up with this neighborhood. Last time I was here, I witnessed local humans walking two blocks out of their way so they wouldn't have to walk down the streets controlled by the vamps.

If he was a local, maybe they were attempting to take

back the area. Or, maybe he was a new acolyte protecting his masters.

The man had to be over six feet tall, with short, curly brown hair. His clothes looked like they had been thrown in a corner wet, and he just put them back on without even washing them. Not uncommon for an acolyte to wear dingy clothes. They were basically slaves after all. Slaves to their vampire masters who decided how they lived and what they wore, if anything at all.

I continued to watch the human and scanned the area looking for vamps. There was a humming sound coming from across the street. The house I found Acadia in seemed to be the source.

One of the best parts about a shifter is my speed. Even in human form I'm much faster than normal people.

After looking around to see if there were any vamps visible, I ran full speed to the guy with the gun. I knocked the gun out of his hand and turned it on him.

"Who are you? What are you doing here?" I kept one eye on the intruder and one eye scanned the street for signs of the enemy.

"Hey, give me that back! I have every right to be here with a gun." This guy didn't seem frightened of me. Huh. Maybe I should have shifted.

"Why do you need a gun in a deserted neighborhood?" The electric noise I heard earlier was louder, it sounded almost like a generator was running. Why would they need electricity here if they abandoned the houses?

"To keep scavengers like you away from our property. Listen man, you really don't want to mess with my employers. If I was you, I'd turn around and forget about this neighborhood." He was warning me? Now that was funny.

I chuckled. "Really? Who do you work for? Vampires, or something?"

His eyes opened wide, and I heard a creak from a door behind me. The sun was still setting, but on this street, the night had already descended. Most of the yards were shadowed in darkness. Stronger vampires could come out now. Newer ones would still feel the effects of the sun for another ten minutes or so.

At the end of the street, I could just make out the last of the sunlight fading on the sidewalk.

"Have you ever met a vampire?" A smile crept along his face, and he crossed his arms over his chest.

I knew a vampire was near. The feeling of death and destruction was always close when a vampire was in the area.

"Yes, I have." I still held the gun.

I spun on my heels as I heard a rustle and knocked the vamp's arm away right before he reached for my neck.

"Tsk, tsk. Romero, you know better than to attack me." The vampire took a step away from me.

"Rico, I didn't realize it was you hassling my acolyte. Give him the gun back. I gave it to him for his own protection. Have you seen all of the riff-raff ravaging poor neighborhoods like ours?" The vampire smirked. He thought he had the upper hand, but he didn't.

"You knew exactly who I was. I just can't believe you thought you could sneak up on me and try to kill me. I should kill you, and your acolyte, where you stand for attempting to attack me."

"You have no proof I was going to hurt you." The sniveling idiot was right, but I wasn't going to tell him that.

Instead I arched an eyebrow and said, "I'll let it go on one condition."

"What?"

"You tell me where the missing girls are. If you aren't involved in their abduction, you will have nothing to worry about."

"I don't know what you're talking about." Romero seemed to be telling the truth.

"Haven't you seen the news?"

"No, once I heard a hurricane was coming I turned off the TV to prepare. Been cleaning up our neighborhood ever since we could get over here." Dangit, if he was telling the truth, we were in the wrong spot.

"What is the noise I heard? Are you running generators?"

"Of course. We don't have electricity here. We are cleaning up the houses and pumping out the water. Can't have the neighbors complaining to the city about not keeping up appearance, now can we?"

"I guess you won't mind me checking out a few of the houses, right?" If he was telling the truth, I needed to know right away.

"You have no authority here. We are not doing anything wrong, so you can't just barge into our houses." Romero narrowed his eyes.

"If you don't have anyone here against their will, I don't care what you are doing right now. You shouldn't have anything to worry about if you're just cleaning up as you say." I heard a noise coming from one of the other houses on this street.

Maybe he was lying after all?

"Let him search. I heard about those missing girls. You believe vampires are responsible?" Another vamp walked out of the house next to where we stood.

"Nick, good to see you. I heard you left town a few weeks

back. Something about not getting along with the queen?" This was interesting.

"You heard wrong. The queen herself asked me to make sure our nice, quiet neighborhood stayed that way. I'm here on official business. Why are you here, Rico?" Nick walked down the stairs, and through the front yard, keeping his eyes peeled on me the entire time.

"We had reports about vampires hanging out in this abandoned neighborhood. Along with humans. I don't recognize your acolyte. How long have you had him?" Granted, I didn't know all of the acolytes, but to give a gun to one meant you trusted him. I should know all of the ones they trusted so much.

"Don't worry, he's legal. Miller here has been with me for ages, haven't you?" Romero looked to his human servant.

"Of course, master. My life is yours and has been for close to two years." The sniveling turd held his hands behind his back and looked to the ground. His knees bent, and then, he stood up straighter. I swear he was about to bow down and worship the blood-sucker.

"Miller, you chose to serve the vampires? They didn't coerce you at all?" I asked all acolytes I came into contact with this question. One just never knew.

"Of course! My master has given meaning to my unworthy life. I take great pleasure in serving him." These acolytes were so brainwashed, it was pathetic.

I sighed heavily and turned my eyes back to Nick.

"I see your mind control works just fine on this one. Have you seen any of the missing girls? We rescued one who swears she ran away from vampires." I wonder if he knew anything at all.

"My queen has personally promised to stake any vampire to the ground just before sunrise if we take anyone against their will. No one would dare defy her orders." Nick was one of the vampires rumored to be on the outs with the vampire queen, Celeste.

I wondered if he was here as punishment. Cleaning up after a hurricane isn't fun. Vampires were very selfish and never did anything to help anyone but themselves. If they were cleaning up, it would be a fitting punishment for going against the queen.

"Good to know. I'm going to start checking out all of the houses, and some of my pack are already here looking around the neighborhood. I would suggest you tell your acolytes to leave them alone. Unless you don't care if my wolves maul them?" I raised an eyebrow and watched Nick try to keep his composure.

"This is our neighborhood. We have a right to protect it as well as ourselves. If your wolves stick their noses where they don't belong, I can't be held responsible for what happens." Romero walked up next to Nick and tried to give me the evil eye. These guys were such drama queens.

"Boys, we are on official business. We have been notified by one of the missing girls there are still some alive who were abducted by vampires. Don't get in my way, or I will be notifying your queen. Do you remember what happened last time I was on official business and a vampire got in my way?" He was killed. I know they knew it.

"Fine, just leave our workers alone. They have a lot of work to finish before the sun comes back up." The sun had barely set and the only one I had interfered with so far was Miller. He wasn't doing anything but watching the street.

"Let's start with this house, shall we?" I walked over to the house Nick came from.

"I wouldn't go in there, if I were you." Nick snickered.

"Really, and why is that?"

"It's breakfast time." Romero shrugged and walked up the steps and inside the house.

"I hope you aren't feeding on innocents for your breakfast." These demons were disgusting.

I didn't want to go in there if they were feeding, but I had to check out the acolytes and make sure they were all here willingly.

Before I even entered the house, I smelled the coppery scent of blood mixed with humans' scents. Female scents to be exact. There was even a hint of vanilla and jasmine underneath the stench.

I prepared myself for girls prostituting themselves out to the blood-suckers. Why so many women, and men, gave their bodies so freely to vampires was one of the great mysteries of this world.

It didn't matter how good the sex was, how could anyone allow a demon to suck their blood?

"Oh, Buddha! What is this? Are you running a bordello right in town?" The sight in front of me made me want to puke. Young, pretty girls dressed in nothing more than lingerie were all over the room.

Some were up against the walls with vampires drinking from their necks. While others were sitting in the laps of vampires. The only thing stopping me from puking was the fact all of the men still had their clothes on. I hated to think what this room would look like in another few minutes.

"Alright, that's enough. Leave the girls alone." I really didn't want to watch one more minute of a vampire version of *The Best Little Whorehouse in Louisiana*.

"Girls, do any of you know of any humans taken against their will?" I didn't see any of them struggling against the fangs in their necks. Most had looks of pure pleasure on their face. These all must be here willingly.

None of them looked at me. Either they were ashamed of their behavior, or they were trained to look at the ground. I'm betting the latter.

"Girls, I need someone to answer my questions." There is no way six missing girls wouldn't have been seen somehow, especially if it were vamps who abducted them.

One girl who appeared to be around twenty-five looked up into my face. "My masters would never force a girl to do anything. We all volunteered because we love our vampire masters. How dare you accuse them of such things!"

Another crossed her arms over her chest and narrowed her eyes while her nostrils flared. "You should die for your impertinence! No one makes such claims against our family and gets away with it!"

Nick had a smug look on his face. "As you can see, all of our women are very happy to live with us. They are getting exactly what they want, as are we. No one is getting hurt. Are you my loves?" Nick rubbed his hand down the arm of the closest girl to him.

She looked up at him with love in her eyes. Or maybe it was crazy eyes, not really sure. She was a petite blonde wearing a pink teddy and matching high heels. She tilted her head and invited Nick to bite her.

When he sunk his fangs into her neck, I had to turn my head. My stomach churned with revolt. I wanted nothing more than to get as far away from here as soon as possible. However, this would be the perfect cover for hiding those girls. I needed to search the house.

"Romero, do you want to accompany me on this search?" I wanted one of the vamps close in case I did find the missing girls. He would be a great target to lash out at should I discover them breaking the accords.

"Of course. There is nothing here for you, unless you

want to partake in some blood? We have more women in the rooms upstairs, if you like such an experience?" Romero knew he disgusted me. I think he took pleasure in turning my stomach.

I searched each and every room. There was even a trap door in the mudroom off the side of the kitchen. It led to a flooded tunnel.

"Is this what you are trying to clean up? Your tunnels?" It made sense. They would need to get the water out of there as quickly as possible if they wanted to be able to use these tunnels at any time.

"Yes, as well as the debris across the yards and streets." Romero led me down the upstairs hallway and opened each door for me to look inside.

"What do the surrounding neighbors think? You have vamps and acolytes moving through here at all times of the night. Sometimes, there is no activity for weeks. Don't they question you all?" I had wondered how they were able to keep the neighbors from discovering who they were.

"Most think we are voodoo practitioners so they stay away. Some think we run party services, and others think we're a rock band. I like to keep them guessing." When Romero smiled, there was nothing comforting about it. His fangs protruded through his mouth, and his eyes narrowed with red pinpricks. He was the quintessential vampire.

There was nothing in the house except for women giving their necks and bodies willingly. It was the most disgusting display of depravity I have ever witnessed. Even the vampire queen herself never allowed such displays when I would visit her. Did she know, in her absence, these vamps allowed everyone to watch?

I needed to keep moving. Once I was back at Jenna's, I

would ask her if we could put on some wholesome cartoons. Anything to get those images out of my head.

After I searched Nick's house, I went next door. Thankfully, it was empty.

I pulled out my cell phone and dialed Luke. "Luke, I found vamps, but it was the regular group. They have plenty of volunteers here. If they can be believed, they don't know anything about any missing girls, other than what's been on the news. Have you found anything?"

"So far just acolytes draining their tunnels of the rainwater. Don't you find it odd they're cleaning up this neighborhood when they supposedly abandoned it a few months ago?"

"Luke, I think they are just trying to keep their options open for locations. If they don't drain the water, the tunnels would probably collapse. Which could cause issues with the foundations of the house, depending on where they made their tunnels. Either way, I think it's a punishment for the lead vampires here." I wasn't sure what was going on, but punishment was most likely part of the equation.

However, I doubted they had the missing girls. They didn't need them.

"Have you heard from Damien? Maybe his crew got lucky?" Luke had a point, I hadn't heard from Damien yet.

It could mean they were in the middle of a fight. Or, it could just mean they didn't have anything to report yet. I hoped it was the former since we had no luck here.

"Alright, round up your men and prepare them for patrols. I'll call Damien and see if he has any news. If he doesn't answer, we'll all head over there and help." If Damien didn't answer, I hoped it meant he was in the middle of killing a horde of vampires.

I hung up with Luke and dialed Damien.

Damien answered right away. "Hey, Rico. Any news?"

"No. How about you?"

"It appears some vamps have nested here in the past but not right now. They might have been sent packing when the storm hit. Either way, no sign of missing girls." Dang it! I truly hoped Damien had them or at least their scent.

"Alright, spread out over the city. I want a search of the entire area, grid by grid. We have to check everything." This was not going to be easy.

"Hold up, Jose has something." Damien put his phone on speaker, and I was able to hear his conversation with Jose.

"Damien, I found something which makes me believe they were here. No one is here now, but I found a purse with ID inside. It belongs to the girl who was seen floating on the news report, Melissa. If her purse is here, I'm guessing she was held here until they killed her." Jose had struck gold.

"Rico, did you hear that?" Damien asked.

"Yes, keep searching the entire place. See if you can pick up on some scents. Maybe we can use them to lead us to the girls." At least we had a lead now. This was the best news we'd had since Lisa showed up.

17

JENNA

"Joseph, any news?" I was going stir-crazy sitting here waiting for an update. Rico and the guys left a few hours ago and not one word so far.

"Not yet, Jenna. Don't worry. No news is good news, in this case. If they had found the girls, we would have heard something by now. If they were in trouble, we would have heard something by now. So this just means they are still searching and haven't found anything yet." Joseph really needed to learn what good news meant.

"Joseph, no news in this case isn't good. It's not bad, but it's not good either. It just means those poor girls are still in the hands of the vamps. Maybe we should call Rico? Or Damien? Or someone?" I bit my lower lip to keep myself from screaming out my frustration.

Joseph pulled his cell out of the back pocket of his jeans. "Ahh, speak of the devil. Rico just texted me."

"And?" Indie was just as anxious as I was.

"He's on his way here now. They didn't find the girls, yet. They did find some evidence of where they were being kept before the hurricane. Maybe it will be enough to catch the scent. Hard to say." Joseph put his phone away after responding to Rico.

"Alright, what's the plan for tonight? Should be split up and join the different groups out on patrol? Now that we have our magical charms we should be able to help." Kat was looking forward to kicking some vampire butt, just as I was.

Joseph chuckled. "Whoa, calm down. I doubt Rico is going to let you out tonight. During the day he might be open to you helping with the search but not at night. Too many vamps out and about lately. Since traffic is way down the vampires are out in droves. It's better for them when there aren't as many people on the streets."

"Why is that? I don't get it." How could fewer people on the streets be good for them? I would think they'd want to hide in the throngs of people.

"Not as many witnesses. We usually see people with low blood count show up in the hospital. The vamps are careful not to drain them dry, but they do like to taste different necks whenever they can." That was sick.

"How do you know?" He didn't work in the hospital, as far as I knew.

"I have friends who work in the local ER. They tell me about the cases of low blood count and punctures on necks and shoulders." Joseph was seriously connected in town. I bet he knew where all of the bones were buried, so to speak.

"Do you know all of the local gossip? How do you know all of these people and get them to tell you things?" Records from the ER were confidential and protected by Federal laws.

"One of the spells I get from my witch friend is a truth potion. I can get people to open up and tell me anything I want. As long as they are mundanes. The spells don't work on the paranormal." What a great spell! I wondered if Joseph could get me some of those.

"One of these days you are going to have to start telling us some stories. I bet you could write a book and publish it as fiction while telling the real story of New Orleans! People would buy it up so fast! It could all be the truth too." I shook my head and chuckled, thinking about what we have learned so far.

"Shoot, we could write a book on our experiences and call it *New Orleans Magic* and sell it as fiction. I bet it would make us lots of money." Now Sam was thinking about writing a book of our experiences? This could be good.

"You can call the series, *The Voodoo Dolls*! Make it Urban Fantasy, and you can write about all of our adventures and exploits since having learned magic is real! No one would suspect it was true." I liked this idea. We all needed to get together and write this book.

"You wouldn't be the first to do so. I bet you'd be surprised how many paranormal and urban fantasy authors are writing about actual experiences." Ohh, I wonder if Joseph knew any of them.

It would be so cool to meet others who have experienced what we have. If for no other reason than to have someone to talk to about it all. It's not like I can go to a shrink and tell them I almost lost my life to a blood-sucking demon of the night. Hello? Padded room for one, please.

Someone knocked at the door, and I jumped in my seat. My mind was a million miles from NOLA, and the noise actually frightened me.

Kat got up and answered it. "Rico, come on in. Give us an update."

Once we were all settled on the sofa and chairs Rico began telling us of his experience. "Jenna, this is why I don't want you out there. Could you really handle seeing what I saw tonight?"

"I would have puked. No question about it." Indie looked a little green under the gills.

I couldn't blame her. "I would have too."

"I think we all would have run screaming from that den of iniquity. I doubt any normal human would have been able to stomach such a scene." Kat shook her head and turned a very pale shade of human.

"Alright. I think we all need to replace those images with something fun. What do you say to pirates? Our favorite Pirate Jack movie has a new release coming soon, we could have a marathon and get all caught up!" This was something we all needed. Even Rico seemed a bit upset about the evening.

Sam had been quiet up until this point. "I'm all for some hot pirate action, but what about the missing girls? Is there anything we can do at all for them?"

"Yes, you can stay home and let my pack continue searching. Tomorrow, if you want, you can join us in the hunt during the day. My guys are doing a grid search and until we check every inch of the city, we have no clue where they may have gone." Rico sat next to me on the couch and put his arm on the top of the sofa behind my head. It kinda reminded me of high school. Smooth move. Not!

"I think we can do it. Who's up for popcorn?" Indie jumped up and ran into the kitchen. She loved popped corn with movies. Of course, it was organic popcorn, so much healthier than the stuff most people ate. I only hoped we still had some black licorice left.

We all raised our hands for popcorn, even Joseph and Rico.

Sam retrieved the DVD's and set them up.

"Who wants a soda?" I asked when I got up and went to the kitchen.

"Me."

"I do."

It looked like everyone wanted popcorn and soda. I grabbed enough cans from the fridge for everyone and rummaged through the cabinets to find the last bag of black licorice.

Indie gave me her usual evil eye when she saw me remove the bag of black licorice. Don't get me wrong, I like to eat healthy, just not ALL the time.

"I need to make a trip to the nearest Price Club soon. Does anyone know which ones are open? I'm thinking of going tomorrow." I pulled out my phone to do a search while we waited for the popcorn.

Sam wasn't going to start the movie until we were all sitting in the living room and situated with drink and snacks.

"Oh! I have a few items to add to the list." Sam jumped up from her spot on the floor and grabbed a pen and notepad.

I scrolled through the website to see which stores were open. "Looks like it's gonna be a road trip. Rico, you guys need anything while I'm a few hours away?"

"Really? Which location are you planning to head to?"

"I think I'm going to have to head up to Jackson in order to get an open location." It was over a three hour drive each way. If I took the van and filled up on our usual stuff and helped the pack out, it would be worth it. I would just lose an entire day.

"What about Mobile? The storm didn't hit them nearly as hard as it did us. Is that location open?" Joseph asked.

"I'll look. I wasn't thinking about going East. I thought

going north, away from the gulf would be the best." I scrolled through my phone looking for any information on the Mobile location.

"Yup, they are open. Looks like business as usual for Mobile, Alabama. Good, they're about an hour closer." I could leave at first light and still be back before dark if I went there. Plus, my favorite coffee shop had a sister store there. I could pick up some freshly roasted and ground coffee beans for all of us.

"Alright, I'll go first thing tomorrow. Anyone want to help me? Joseph, you guys need anything at all? I'd be happy to shop for you as well." I owed them big. This would be a simple way of starting to pay back my debt.

"How about Indie and I make the trip? The pack really could use a lot of items. We might even want to bring one of the guys with us to help with lifting." I wasn't surprised Joseph wanted to go with Indie and not me. In fact, if Indie was open to this arrangement, I would be happier to help search for the missing girls.

"Sure, I can help. I love Price Club shopping. Girls, just be sure to write out anything you could possibly want. Who knows when we'll get another chance to go back, or when our location will open up." Indie sat on the floor in front of Joseph who was in one of our recliners.

Joseph began massaging Indie's shoulders as soon as the lights went down and the movie started. Interesting. Were they already moving forward? Both of them seemed rather relaxed with his hands on her. Like they were already a couple and massaging shoulders was a regular thing for them. I had never seen him rub her shoulders, but that didn't mean they hadn't done this before.

18

JENNA

"*R*ico, it's light out. How can I help today?" I called Rico the second I woke up.

No one other than Indie was up yet. She was getting ready to head out with Joseph for the day. Today was supposed to be our day to help search for the storm girls.

The media had started calling the missing girls "The Storm Girls," even though most of them went missing before the storm. With two dead bodies discovered and one who ran to my store, there were still five missing girls in total. I wasn't naïve enough to think we would rescue them all, but I hoped they were still alive. Of course I prayed they would all make it, but I had to prepare myself for what would probably happen.

"Jenna, it isn't even eight o'clock yet. You really want to get up this early and get started?" Rico sounded groggy, like I'd woken him up.

"Dude, you should have had at least a good six hours of sleep if you went straight home after the movies." It wasn't even midnight when they left. We only watched two of the four movies. Everyone was falling asleep.

"I didn't go straight to bed. I have a pack to run as well as an investigation. It was after five when I finally got to bed." Oh wow! Rico totally needed more sleep. I can't believe he even answered the phone.

"Sorry. Go back to sleep. I've got some things to do around town anyway. I'll get my errands going and meet you when you get to town. Call me before you leave home."

"Thanks, Jenna. Talk to you soon." He hung up, and I got out of bed to see if coffee was brewing yet.

"Indie, you didn't start the coffee maker?" I stared into the empty coffee pot and had a tough time understanding why she didn't turn it on.

"We're grabbing some coffee on our way out. I thought for sure you would still be in bed. These past few days have been tough, and you don't need to be up yet, do you?" Little did Indie know, but I had some plans of my own this morning.

"I couldn't sleep anymore so I decided to get up instead of tossing and turning in my bed. Have a great day shopping and hanging with your new boyfriend." They had to be together now, right?

"We aren't dating. For the moment, we are keeping it friendly." Indie's eyes turned down and she sighed.

"Indie, if you want him, you might have to make the first move. He's totally into you, so I don't know why you aren't a couple yet."

"It's because we want to take it slow. The way our family has integrated into their pack would make it very difficult on all of us if there was a break-up. I'm sure it's the same with you and Rico. You two are totally into each other but haven't made the plunge, right?" She had a point.

"Okay, I get it. Just promise me one thing."

"Sure, anything."

"Don't make a voodoo doll out of Joseph if things go downhill, no matter the reason for your break-up. Can you promise me?" There was no way it would go down well with the pack if Indie created a Joseph voodoo doll. They would go ballistic. Shoot, I would too.

Indie chuckled and smiled at me. "Jenna, I wouldn't do that to anyone in the pack. We have to keep up our relationships with them, no matter what happens. Our lives kinda depend on them now."

"I agree wholeheartedly. Which is why I haven't let anything happen with Rico. I couldn't handle a bad break-up with him. I doubt our family would be able to handle it either."

"True. Alright, let's agree to keep things slow with the guys and not jump into anything until both parties are in love. Deal?" Indie stuck her hand out.

I grabbed it and shook. "Deal. I think this is one of our smarter arrangements."

"Me too."

A knock sounded at the door, and Indie's face lit up like the sun. If I wasn't mistaken, she was already on her way to being in love with the guy.

The second I was ready for the day I headed out. Kat and Sam were still in bed, and I hadn't heard from Rico yet. I was on my own for the first time in a while.

Before meeting Rico and his pack, I used to spend one morning a week strolling through the local farmers market. I enjoyed sampling the different fresh and organic foods while also trying out different smoothies or coffee drinks. Today wouldn't be like those days.

It was going to be a bit more exciting. Once I was in line for coffee at my favorite shop, I checked my purse to ensure I had the charms. Hidden away, inside a pouch, was each of the magic stones, including the red stone of death. I also had on my matching jewelry and a couple extra spells on my wrist.

Since it was still light out, I didn't expect to encounter any vampires. Acolytes were a whole other story. If one attacked me, I would defend myself.

There was a storage facility next to one of the more popular graveyards here in town. I know the pack hadn't hit the center of the city yet. It would be tough to stick it out here during the storm, but if you were on the top floor of a storage facility, you would have been safe. Those places don't have windows. What better way to hide during the day?

My plan was to just check this place out and see if I could locate acolytes. If they were there, then vampires would be too.

All I had to do was scope out the place, I wasn't about to storm the castle, even if the girls were there. I learned my lesson, I think.

After I took another inventory of my supplies, I took off and headed to Castle Storage. The morning was quiet and really beautiful. Sunshine and a nice breeze off the lake made it an enjoyable walk. The buses had resumed, but their schedule was off. Walking gave me a chance to think about what I would do when I arrived.

The storage facility was one of those you needed a code to get inside of. It was possible to climb the back fence, but there were also security cameras all over the place. This wasn't the time to get caught breaking in.

When I walked up to the facility, I could see the brick walls surrounding the entire place had seen some water damage. The storm must have caused a flood in this neighborhood, but the water line was only up a few inches on the wall.

The little office next to the metal gate had an open sign in its window. A great idea popped into my head.

I opened the door and plastered a smile on my face. "Hi, there! Beautiful day today, isn't it?"

"Sure is. How can I help you?" The young man behind the counter smiled at me. He had black hair and was wearing jeans and t-shirt. I would have expected a polo shirt, at least. But I supposed he was probably still cleaning up too.

"I wanted to see if you had any second floor units available and what kind of damage your facility took from the hurricane." This was the plan to get me inside the storage facility. Pretty ingenious, if you ask me.

"We didn't take a direct hit here, so the damage was minimal. We only had about two inches of water build up. The facility is built up a foot above ground, so none of the units sustained any damage."

"Impressive. I own a shop in town, and we spent hours getting everything off the ground floor before the worst of the storm hit. I was thinking maybe we should store some of the overstock up on your second floor so it won't be so much work for us when the next storm comes through." Actually, this is a really good idea. I'd have to discuss this with my sisters later today.

"We can't guarantee no damage will occur in a storm, but if you're on the second floor, your chances are much better. Since it is safer, we charge extra for second floor units. What size were you looking for?" The attendant came around from behind the counter and carried a large, round key ring with what had to be over thirty keys.

"I'm not sure. Can we look at the different sizes and

prices so I can figure it out?" I only thought of this idea on the way here, I didn't have time to think about sizing.

"Sure, come with me. What's your name? You look familiar." The guy was checking me out. He was only a few years older than me, but I doubt I knew him.

"I'm Jenna. What's your name?"

"Scott. Nice to meet you...Wait? Are you a Voodoo Doll?" Scott stopped before opening the door and turned around with excitement evident on his face.

"Yes, I am. Are you a fan of our music?" This was going to be fun if he was a fan.

"Of course! Who isn't? I went to your concert at the Bikini Beach Bar a few months back. That was epic! Can I get an autograph? Oh! And a picture with you? My friends will never believe I actually met you!" He pulled out his cell phone and was ready for a selfie.

"Sure. What do you want me to autograph?" It wasn't too often I came across fans outside of a club or our store.

"Here, let's take a picture first. I want to post it all over my social media! Then, I guess you could sign my notepad?" He stood next to me with his phone in camera mode and began taking pictures of us.

"Thanks! My friends are going to flip out when they see these!" The guy instantly tweeted and posted in Facebook. He probably posted in a few other sites as well.

He walked back to the counter and reached over for his notebook.

"Here, on the inside cover. Can you sign this; 'For my favorite fan, Scott Walton. Love, Jenna.'"

I giggled thinking about who my actual favorite fan was. It certainly wasn't this guy, even though he was really nice.

Would Rico care about this kind of stuff?

After I signed his notebook, we went out the side door.

"We have a few spots open in this section. Both are on the smaller side, but we do get people moving out all of the time. If you need something larger, I can put you on a wait list and call when we get a move-out notice." Scott opened up the door to stairwell and I followed him up.

Something was off. The charm on my wrist warmed a bit as did the one around my neck. Joseph said they would do that if a paranormal creature, besides the pack, was close by. Since it didn't do this when I was in the office with Scott, he had to be fully human.

No one knew where I was. I had to at least text Rico my location, just in case.

I pulled out my phone and was texting Rico when Scott turned around and grabbed my phone. "Hey, what the heck? I was just texting my boyfriend."

"There is a no getting away policy. Thanks for making this so easy. I hope you enjoy your new home!" Scott waved his hand to the side like Vanna White and showcased several closed, but not locked, storage units. They were larger than he said earlier.

"What is this? I don't understand." I looked around and noticed one door as it began to roll up.

"Help! Please help us!" Some girl screamed from behind a locked door.

"Who are you?" I backed up to toward the door hoping to get away.

Scott reached out and grabbed my arm. My protective charms only defended against magic, not against a human grabbing me.

Lucky for me, I had other gifts to defend myself with.

I kicked him in the family jewels, and he gasped in pain and bent over. I pulled his head down on my knee and felt his nose break against my kneecap. Blood flowed on my pant leg.

"Great, another pair of jeans destroyed. Dude, you better not be who I think you are. I hope for your sake you're just a crazed fan who has gone too far." Even though there was at least one girl screaming, I had to get outside and call for back-up. Rico would kill me if I tried to rescue her on my own, even if vampires weren't involved.

My phone had been thrown across the ground. I ran to grab it. When I stood up to leave, someone grabbed me from behind.

"Ahh, new blood. Feisty too. I love a challenge!" The guy behind me was seriously strong. I tried to get his hand off me, but it wouldn't budge.

He leaned in and put his mouth on my neck. Something on me glowed and shot the guy back against one of the roll-up doors before he could sink his fangs into me. He slid to the ground, and his eyes rolled to the back of his head. I hoped he would be out for a while.

"Huh, I didn't know the magic would be so strong. Awesome!" With the phone in my hand, I turned to run to the exit.

Another vampire blocked the door.

Where did he come from?

19

JENNA

"**S**orry, you won't be leaving here today." The smirk on his face chilled my blood.

I had several defensive spells on my body and some in my bag. I wanted to try the stones first.

I reached into the pocket holding the stones. I pulled out a handful while I kept my eyes on the vamp by the door.

"Sorry, I have plans." I threw without even looking to see what color I grabbed.

Stink! I hope it wasn't the red one.

A violet rock hit the vamp's chest and bounced down to the ground in front of him. A cloud of purple haze surrounded him. If he had been human, it would have choked him. Since vampires didn't breathe air, it just blocked my vision of him.

He was still standing in the doorway, I turned hoping to find another exit on this floor. There had to be an elevator.

Scott was attempting to stand up, and I punched him as hard as I could in the gut. He doubled over and fell to the ground holding his stomach. I could see the pain in his face. Tears streamed down his cheeks and his lips trembled. *Good.*

The girl was still screaming for help. Another door rolled up, and three more vamps walked out and blocked my path.

I still held my phone in my hand. Getting the text out to Rico was important. I took another rock and threw it at the three vamps. This time, a pink force field came up.

The force field only worked for a minute. This was my chance to text Rico. I put my thumb on the home button and unlocked my phone. The text I started was still on my screen. I typed in the location and told him there were at least 5 vampires here with some humans.

I hit the send button, but with all of the metal the message was having a hard time sending.

"No, no, no! Come one! You have to send."

The vampire I left by the door in the purple haze was laughing. The pink field in front of me was going to drop at any moment. I had no choice. I pocketed my phone and hoped the message would get out.

"The little doll has magic after all. I thought you and your sisters were mundanes? Where did you get magic?" The purple haze vamp narrowed his eyes at me and stalked closer and closer.

I couldn't use the red stone here, it would kill me too. There were still two more colored stones in my hand. One wouldn't work on a vampire. It was designed to put the target in a bubble and suck the air out. I doubted it would hold the vamp. The other... might work. It also might hurt me.

Pulling the yellow stone out of my palm, I threw it right at the vamp's chest. He reached out his right hand and grabbed the stone. "What's this?"

I heard a loud kaboom before the concussion of the power not only threw him against the wall, it also threw me back against the wall. I was too close when I threw it.

My head hit the wall hard and bounced down. "Ow! That's gonna leave a bump." I put my hand to the back of my head and rubbed. A bump had already started to form.

Strong hands grabbed me and yanked me up. I secretly pocketed the red stone and fisted the brown in my hand.

"What's in your hand?" The vampire opened my fist and pulled the brown stone out.

I kept my mouth shut and narrowed my eyes.

If he bit me, would the necklace repulse him like it did the other one?

"Girl, you better tell me what this stone does. Or you will be my lunch." The vampire tightened his grip on my shoulders. One of his clawed fingers dug into my left shoulder.

I tried to stifle the scream on my lips from the pain. It came out as a whimper. Not the greatest but better than a scream. They probably got off on making girls scream.

"Last chance. What is this?" He held the stone up to my face between his fingers.

"It's a magical charm." My snark was going to get me in real trouble one day.

He roared. "I know it's a magical charm! What does it do?" His fangs protruded, and he licked his lips when he stared at my pulsing vein.

"It doesn't work on vampires. It's designed to encapsulate a human and suck the air out of the bubble." At least, I think that's what the brown one did.

Scott stood up and slowly made his way to me. "You stupid cow! If you would have just gone along with everything, you could have performed your music for my masters, and they would have taken great care of you!"

"Master, she is the lead singer of The Voodoo Dolls. She

came here looking for a storage unit. I brought her as a gift for you." Scott bowed down and grunted from the pain.

"I know who she is, you fool! I told you to stop picking out women for us! We can't afford to bring any more attention to our little coven." The vampire holding me pushed Scott to the ground.

"I'm sorry. I know how much you love her signing. I thought she would be perfect." Scott stayed on the ground.

"She is dating the alpha of the local wolf pack, you fool! Someone will notice her absence. The entire pack has her scent! They will find us. Another perfect hideout ruined! You can't even follow simple instructions!" The vampire threw the brown stone at Scott.

I watched in horror as a bubble circled his head and cut off his oxygen supply.

"Nathan, that's a waste of perfectly good blood. You know we hate to eat from the body once it's already dead. You really should have let us have him instead of suffocating him," one of the vampires, who had been behind the pink field, exclaimed.

"Alexy, go right ahead and have him. The bubble is only covering his head and neck. His arms are free. Hurry before he dies from asphyxiation." Nathan's laugh was more like a maniacal serial killer. The hairs on my arms stood on end.

Something vibrated in my jacket pocket.

My phone! The text must have just been sent. Thank goodness! I needed to stall them.

It would take Rico an hour to get here. If any of his pack were in town, I could be rescued sooner.

"You might as well let me go. If you leave town now, you might have a chance to survive." Rico would never let them survive, but they didn't know it.

"We have some time. Your boyfriend won't find you. I

doubt anyone will even think you're missing until after nightfall." Nathan was very wrong.

"Actually, I'm supposed to meet Rico in less than an hour. If I don't show up, he will come searching for me. I don't care how many you have on your side, you won't be able to survive against him and his pack. They're the best. Even the local vampire queen doesn't mess with him."

"Right, and I bet you have a bridge to sell me? Girl, no one messes with a vampire queen. Especially one as old as Celeste." If these guys know Celeste, they must be acting with her approval.

"Really? You know Celeste? I guess this means she approves of your kidnapping the storm girls? Those screams, they're from the missing girls, aren't they?" I knew it had to be the ones I was looking for. I just never thought I would stumble upon them this close to my home.

"No, Celeste ostracized me years ago. I have my own coven now. I'm really not too sorry you stumbled upon us." He had to raise his voice as the girls began screaming again. This time I could make out at least two distinct voices.

I heard Scott's body slump to the ground. He had four vamps drinking from his arms. I didn't know if he died from the blood loss or the lack of oxygen. The bubble around his head popped after he fell to the ground.

"Did you just drink the life out of your own acolyte?" They didn't even give him their blood. They must have really been upset with him.

"He disobeyed too many times. Those last two missing girls were his idea. We should have left them alone. It brought too much attention to us." One of the vampires who had fed on Scott licked his tongue and drew closer to me.

"Stop! Don't even think about drinking my blood. I'm covered in a protective spell. Ask your friend who already tried to sink his fangs into my neck." I nodded to the guy standing off to the side who stayed quiet. Although, his fangs were extended and his red eyes stayed focused on me.

"She's right. She has some sort of magic on her. You can grab her, but you can't bite her. I was thrown against the wall and received enough of an electrical shock, it was almost enough to restart my heart." I didn't realize he had such a violent reaction to the magic protecting me.

"It will wear off. All spells do. When it does, I am going to be the first to sink my fangs into your pristine neck and drink until I've had my fill." The vampire against the wall licked his lips and stepped closer to me.

"I doubt it. Rico will be here before the magic wears off." If I could just get them to leave. Their smell is on me so Rico and the entire pack can track them down easily.

My phone began to buzz in my pocket.

"What's that noise?" Vampires had excellent hearing.

"Her phone. Check her for a phone." Alexy grabbed my arm and yanked me away from Nathan's grasp.

Several sets of hands felt all over my body. Nathan checked my jacket pocket last. He pulled out the phone.

"She got a text message." He read the message and threw my phone to the corner of the room where it burst into too many pieces to repair.

"Hey! That's a very expensive phone! It's going to cost me about seven hundred dollars to replace it! You owe me for the broken phone." I was pulling against the hand holding me.

"Doll face, you won't be alive much longer, I would worry more about how much time you have left than a stupid phone." Nathan ran his finger along my neck.

"I think you and I will both enjoy her neck. She smells

sweet." Nathan leaned in and sniffed along my neck and shoulder.

"Gross! Get away from me, you creep!" I kicked out and got him in his kneecap. I heard a crack which must have seriously hurt.

Nathan fell to the ground and screamed, "You'll pay for that!"

"Not likely. It's more likely I will watch as Rico and his pack tear you and your coven apart, limb from limb. It won't be the first time, either." I smirked.

Nathan stood up and backhanded me so hard I flew a few feet away. While it hurt enough to bring tears to my eyes, it also pushed me out of the path of the vamps. I jumped up and made for the exit.

One vampire stood in my way. The rest were behind me laughing.

"You are not worth waiting for. Bob, just kill her. She's too much of a handful. When her phone beeped, it was a message from the local pack alpha, he's on his way here. We need to grab our stuff and go before they get here."

"I want to leave them a little present." Nathan was really stupid if he thought killing me would stop Rico. It would only enrage him and cause the entire pack to hunt these guys down until they were all dead.

I turned one of my defensive bracelets on right before I plowed into Bob the vampire.

Bob grabbed me and immediately let go. I could see the arc from the electricity my charm generated. He fell to the ground and flopped like a fish out of water. Without slowing, I ran through the door.

Right before I made it to the bottom, another vampire tried to grab me from behind. He suffered the same fate as

Bob. I could smell his flesh as it burned from touching the electrical field which surrounded my body.

When I opened the door, the vampire's hand was in the path of the sun. It sizzled before he could move his hand back into the shadows. Without even thinking, I grabbed him and struggled to bring him into the light.

He screamed as my electricity shot through his entire being. It only took a couple of steps, and he was half-way in the sunlight.

The vampire's body burst into flames and almost burned my hands. If I hadn't had my protective charm bracelet on, the magical flames would have burned my body as well.

I was breathing hard when someone wrapped their arms around me from behind. Without even thinking, I grabbed their arm and threw them over my shoulder. A body thunked against the storage facility wall.

My eyes popped open wide when I realized I had thrown a human guy into the wall. I didn't recognize him. He could be another acolyte or just someone in the wrong place at the wrong time.

I had to get out of there before any more acolytes showed up. The electric shock charm must have worn off since the guy didn't get electrocuted when he touched me.

With one last look over my shoulder, I ran as fast as I could out of the place. The vamps destroyed my phone so I couldn't call Rico. My only option was to hightail it back home and hope I made it.

20

JENNA

I made it as far as Uncle Wong's before I almost passed out. Distance running was not my thing. Especially at such a fast pace.

"Jimmie... Help!" I collapsed in the entryway of his restaurant.

"Jenna, what happened? Jenna?" Jimmie ran to me and cradled me in his arms.

"Sue, grab my phone and call Rico. Tell him Jenna's here and she passed out." Jimmie picked me up and carried me to the closest booth.

"Water." It was all I could get out.

"Oh! Jenna, you're awake. Good, good. What happened?" Jimmie patted my hand after he laid me down on the red vinyl booth.

"Vampires...storm girls." I continued to try to get my breath.

Someone put a water bottle in my shaky hands. I spilled some trying to get it to my mouth.

"Mmm." The water was sweeter than nectar from the vine.

I continued to sip the water while trying to catch my breath.

The bell over the door signaled someone entering Uncle Wong's.

"Jimmie, is Jenna here? I picked up her scent outside and it's fresh." I recognized Luke's voice.

"Yes! She ran in here out of breath and mentioned vampires and storm girls. I had my wife call Rico." Jimmie sounded so relieved to have one of the wolf-shifters here.

I know I was relieved to have Luke here.

"Hey, Jenna. How are you? Are you ok?" Luke's soft voice could be heard over the loud sound of the vinyl creaking when he slid into the seat across from me.

"I...think...so." Breathing was still tough, but I was finally getting enough air into my lungs.

"Castle Storage. Vampires and storm girls." I opened my eyes and drank some more water.

"I'll call Rico and let him know." Luke pulled out his phone and dialed.

"Rico. I'm at Jimmie's and so is Jenna. She's safe. I smell vamps on her. Multiple." Luke nodded his head while Rico spoke. I couldn't hear what he was saying.

"Of course. I'm not leaving her alone. I think she was at Castle Storage. She said vampires and storm girls in the same breath as the storage place." Luke nodded some more and then hung up.

"Rico was already on his way to the storage place with some of the pack before coming here. You're stuck with me for a while." Luke smiled at me before yelling out, "Jimmie, you're going to have a large party here soon. Once Rico's done he's bringing everyone here. Fire up the wonton soup maker!"

I smiled. Wonton soup did sound fantastic. "I want soup."

Jimmie came out of the back with a tray. When he set it before me, I relaxed my shoulders and sighed. "Wonton soup and tea. Drink up. It will help you feel better."

"Thanks, Jimmie."

"Luke, can you call my sisters and let them know I'm here. My cell phone broke. I'll have to get another one." After I took a couple sips of the soup, I was done.

"I need a nap. Either using those spells took a lot out of me, or the entire experience of this morning did." Jimmie's restaurant was slow, so I laid on the bench and dozed.

RICO

"When is she ever going to learn?" I couldn't believe the trouble Jenna could get into. Even in the middle of the morning. I'm just grateful she was able to get out of the place before her magical charms wore off.

I wanted to head straight to Uncle Wong's and check on her, but I had to go to the storage facility first. Jenna was safe and protected. Those poor girls were not. I just hoped the vamps left me some evidence.

"Damien, how long until your group arrives at the storage lot?" I was on the phone now with Damien who had a van full of anxious wolves. Everyone wanted to rip into a vampire.

"Almost there, maybe ten more minutes. Have you heard from Jenna?"

"Luke called. He's with her. They're at Uncle Wong's. He's going to stay with her until we are done with the vamps." I hoped they were still there packing, but if Jenna got away, they have most likely left town already.

"I'll see you there." Damien hung up, and I focused on

the road. As soon as I got her message this morning, I was out the door and barreling down the road. Damien rallied the troops and followed not long after.

Once I arrived at the storage facility, I parked and waited. The proper thing to do would be to wait for my back-up, since Jenna was safe and sound, but my wolf was itching to come out and play. He rarely got out anymore.

I needed to take a day or two and go camping some-where. Maybe even find a place I could stay in wolf form for a couple of days. It wasn't good to hold your inner wolf back for long. If he didn't get out regularly, he ended up forcing his way out. Which never went over well.

I rolled my window down as I waited, and the breeze blew in a scent I knew all too well. Vampires.

My wolf was screaming to get out. Damien was almost here, it wouldn't hurt to shift and run the perimeter.

I got out of my car and locked it. After I pocketed the key, I casually walked to a large magnolia tree. I took a quick look to make sure no one was watching and then shifted.

My wolf sighed his pleasure at being let out.

It was easy to hop the fence in wolf form. I began running the inside perimeter and sniffing for any familiar scents.

Halfway through the facility I picked up vanilla, cherry blossoms, and a hint of cinnamon. My wolf went nuts... Jenna. I had lost control. The wolf followed her scent, no matter what I said.

Come on, we have to wait for backup. You know this. Jenna's safe. Let's just focus on the perimeter.

My wolf wasn't listening to me. Honestly, it was my own fault for keeping him leashed up for so long. It felt really good to be in wolf form and searching for vampires to tear apart.

Maybe, just maybe, my wolf wasn't totally uncontrolled. It could be I wanted to rip them apart as well.

I stalked through the small walkways between the buildings, following a scent I would know anywhere. I found it to be weak, meaning she hadn't been here for a while, and she probably wasn't in this part of the complex. The wind was blowing her scent all over me.

I growled as soon as I crossed a male scent. Human. I moved even faster.

It looked like I was in the front of the complex. I could see the office from my location. Jenna's scent was stronger, but it was mixed with two males now.

"Grrr." *Mate.*

My wolf recognized Jenna as our mate. Any other male scent mixed with hers would cause my primal instincts of possession and protection to kick in. If those human men hurt her, I doubt I could stop my wolf from tearing them apart.

Vampires, at least five distinct scents of death.

Jenna's scent now intermingled with three of the vampires.

There was also a trail of human female scents moving away from the building. I wanted to follow those scents since I knew Jenna wasn't here, but my wolf ignored me. It wanted, no it needed, to follow Jenna's scent and see what happened.

Her scent led to a door, which was open. The door opened up to a set of stairs going up. Under my paws was dust. I lowered my head and took a deep sniff. *Vampire ash.*

Good job, Jenna. At least one down now.

I continued to scent the air as I prowled up the steps. My nose picked up Jenna's fragrance mixed with blood.

The hackles on my back rose, and I howled. They had

hurt Jenna enough to draw blood. None of them would survive, not even the acolytes.

I heard at least ten wolves respond to my howls. My pack had arrived. Good.

I think the vampires had all left. If those other scents I discovered, before coming into the building, were the missing storm girls, I could send half my pack after them while I continued to investigate what happened here.

I heard someone running up the stairs, it wasn't a wolf.

"Rico, what happened? Are they gone?" Damien ran into the hallway where I was sniffing out the action from not long ago.

I changed back to my human form so we could communicate.

"Have half the pack follow the female scents leading away from this building. I think those will lead us to the storm girls. Jenna was here and fighting. They drew her blood." I ground my teeth before turning to get a better look at the space.

"Your wolf must be going nuts! How are you controlling it?"

"We know Jenna is safe at Uncle Wong's. I think it's the only thing keeping me sane right now." The wall next to us had scorch marks.

"Look, she must have used some of the charms on them. Does this look like the discharge from an electrical bolt?" I pointed to a wall with a pointed scorch mark in the shape of a lightning bolt.

"Rico, there." Damien pointed down the hall, and I saw more scorch marks on both sides of the walkway.

"She used the force field. Smart girl. I wonder how many vamps she held back?" Even in human form, I could pick up the nuances between vamp scents.

"Three." I continued to smell the area.

"I smell a total of five vamps. She dusted one downstairs. So, four are left." Damien confirmed what I had already sniffed out.

"She was here just a couple of hours ago. How did four vampires leave during the day?" Damien began searching each of the open storage units.

"They had to have a bolt-hole. There's no way they walked out with those girls." In fact, I didn't pick up strong vamp smells when I first noticed their scent. I did scent one human male with them.

"If they didn't walk out the front, is there a back exit?" Damien went further into the building and I followed him.

We each took a side and rolled up each door without a lock.

"Rico, the girls were held in here. I can smell them the strongest in here. Plus, there is a lot of blood drops on the ground in here. They must have fed on them in here, too."

"Poor girls. Had to watch as each was eaten, knowing they would be next." I walked into the unit and looked around.

It was a small space, maybe five feet wide and seven feet deep. With all of the girls in here, there couldn't have been anywhere to look without seeing their fellow captives debased in such a way. The sheer terror, knowing your neck was next.

Did they watch as the two girls were murdered? What horrors they must have experienced.

Disgusted, I walked out of the unit and continued to search. There weren't many open units.

"How did they leave? I don't see a back door." The vamps' stench was everywhere. I needed to find one scent and follow it.

"Damien, I'm going back to my wolf form. I need to isolate one vamp scent and see if I can follow it and find out where they went. For all we know, they're hiding behind one of the locked doors." Wouldn't that be perfect?

"If they were still here, we would sense them." Damien was right. I was reaching for a quick solution.

After I shifted, I picked out one scent and followed it. In my wolf form, my senses were intensified. Even when I was in my human form, I still had excellent senses, but the wolf was a step above. He could pick out one scent and follow it, better than a hound could.

However, a wolf didn't lower himself and put his snout on the ground. We could pick up the scent in the air and keep our heads held high.

The scent I picked up was burnt wood and decayed animals. This was the scent of an older vamp. It also had a tiny hint of cinnamon mixed with it. Was this the blood-sucker who hurt Jenna?

I followed the putrid scent and walked back and forth along the path several times. The vamp, a male, had been in and out of the room of girls several times over the past twenty-four hours or so. Their scent didn't linger much longer than a day.

He also went inside of three, open storage units. Two locked units caught my attentions where the vampire scent seemed to linger. One of them, had multiple vamp scents. I went back and forth between the two locked units. One of them had the smell of death.

It was time to shift back so I could open these two doors.

"Damien, this one smells of death. We have to open the door. The other one, I pointed two doors down, had all of their scents. We need to open both doors."

Jose joined us with bolt cutters and cut both locks before

standing behind me. I pulled off the first broken lock and rolled up the blue metal door.

"Oh! That's disgusting!"

"We have to call the cops. I'm sorry, Rico. I know you wanted to find them all alive." Damien turned around and went outside. I hoped he was calling his detective friend.

Inside the unit was death. Two male bodies had been drained of blood and left to rot. One of the storm girls was there as well.

"I think it's Gina. Can you tell?" I didn't want to go inside, not with the cops coming to investigate.

Jose put a hand over his nose. "Yes, I'm afraid it's Gina."

Gina was the blonde girl who went missing the day of the storm. She and Lisa had both been abducted around the same time, even though they didn't know each other.

The strength of the decay led me to believe they had been dead at least a day, maybe longer. Or, at least one of the bodies had been dead for a day. With all three scents it was difficult to pinpoint time of death.

"Let's open the other door." I walked over to the roll up door where I detected all of the vampire scents.

Jose rolled it up and stepped back.

We both looked at each other and smiled. It was a secret freight elevator.

"This must be how they got out. Is there a tunnel underground? If so, where does it lead?" I needed to grab a few more wolves to join us.

When I walked down the stairs, there were four wolves standing by waiting for my orders.

"All of you, come with me. We found a secret elevator. We need to follow the scent of the demons and pray the rest of the girls are still alive. Damien, you joining us?"

"I'm going to wait for Detective Adams. He said he

would be here in less than ten minutes. Someone needs to stay and let him know what we touched." Damien could handle the cops. If I needed him, I could always call.

We all headed up and went straight for the hidden elevator. It was a good size, but not big enough for all of us in our wolf form. Everyone shifted to their human form before loading in. The elevator went down two levels. There must be an extensive tunnel system here. One we didn't know about.

We splashed down into at least six inches of water. It smelled like a garbage dump. The ammonia scent of decay was very strong and made my nose twitch. I couldn't be sure, but there might even be bodies down here. This was something for the medical examiner to investigate. I wanted to find the vampires.

We walked into a tight tunnel. It was so small no one could stand up straight. We all had to bend over and practically crawl through the loose dirt tunnel. I put both my arms out and had to bend at the elbows because the walls were so close. Good thing none of us were claustrophobic.

"Boss, I see a light up ahead." Jose had taken point, and we followed him single file. I took up the rear.

"Good, but be careful." Something slithered by my leg, and I knew I didn't want to know what it was.

The path snaked its way up above the water level, and once it flattened out, we found ourselves in a garage. There was one van parked and an open spot. The roll up garage door was down.

"Jose, the windows on the van have been blacked out. I think we found our bolt-hole for the vampires." I also observed there were no windows in the garage. Or at least, no visible windows. Junk was piled up against the walls. It could have been covering a window.

"Be careful not to touch anything. Use your shirt to roll the garage door up. The cops will want to investigate here as well. Better not to leave our mark." I had contaminated too many crime scenes in my past. These days, I was extra careful when I could be.

The vampires' stench was fresh. I counted four different rotting corpse scents. Jenna's scent wasn't here, neither were the storm girls. They must have left the storage place in another car.

Once the garage door was rolled up we all walked outside and realized we were less than 2 blocks away from the storage facility. This was a normal neighborhood, one we had not investigated before.

"The vamps chose a great place. Look, it's been foreclosed upon. I bet no one other than our blood-suckers have even been inside the house for weeks." Jose pointed to a sign in the window telling people to stay out. If anyone wanted to view the property, it would be listed for sale shortly.

I lost their scent. They must have had a car here waiting for them. They could be anywhere by now.

"How long have they been using this as their backup? They had to have been the ones who dug the tunnel. It's not like it was an easy feat, either." Jose walked around to the back of the house and yelled out for us to join him.

"They had a small backhoe and worked the tunnel from this side. It probably only took them a week with this equipment." Jose pointed to a small black and white piece of heavy equipment with a giant scoop on a long arm.

"They could have worked their acolytes during the day, and no one would have noticed, not on a bank foreclosure. People tend to ignore contractors coming and going on houses like these." The vampires did something like this at least ten years ago. This group must have thought we wouldn't catch on. They were right.

"We're going to have to pay more attention to contractors and empty houses. Man, we could have found them sooner, if we had been paying better attention." I really screwed up this time. It was imperative I get my head back in the game.

"Jose, get with Joseph when we get back and see if the witches can perform a locating spell. Since we know where they have been, I'm hoping we can find where they are now." Normally, the witches didn't work with us, but with the high profile case of the storm girls, I was betting they would want the vamps found as soon as possible.

"Come on. Let's get back to the storage facility and see if we can find the trail for the girls." I led my guys back through the tunnel.

Damien waited for us next to the elevator on the second floor. "Boss, any sign of them?"

"No. The tunnel is a recent excavation and led to a garage about 2 blocks west of here. The perfect escape route for vampires. They may have left one of their vehicles in the garage of the foreclosed house. I doubt they'll come back, but we should at least put a tracer on it. Just in case."

"Great. Detective Adams has some questions for all of us before we can leave." Damien led me to the Detective who spent the next two hours grilling us.

"How did the elevator get down to a basement? Something like that had to be planned in advance. The concrete looks professional," Jose asked.

"I had one of my guys look into permits for this place. The company hired an elevator crew to put it in a few months back. Apparently, they needed a storage area. They planned to excavate and create a basement storage for the storage company, instead of using any of their units." The detective had already done some great investigative work.

He's someone I wouldn't mind interviewing for my company, if he ever decides to quit working for little pay and no recognition.

"Here, here's my card. Call me if you ever want to look at going into the private sector. Every time we meet, I'm impressed with you." I handed him one of my business cards.

"Thanks, but I would rather stick to working for the government. These cases, where I always meet up with you and your friends, are my least favorite." He pocketed my card. If he wasn't interested, he wouldn't have done so.

Interesting.

"Well, if you change your mind, you know how to find me." Next on my agenda was checking in on Jenna. She had to be going crazy.

22

JENNA

*R*ico leaned over the back of my booth and rubbed my shoulder. "Hey, sleepyhead. Can you wake up?"

My hands instinctively went to my eyes to rub the sleep away. It felt like I had just lain down. "What? What time is it?"

"You've been sleeping for almost three hours. I can't believe you slept through Jimmie's lunch crowd." Rico smiled down on me from his perch on the booth.

"Wow, I feel like I just laid down. I can't believe I slept so long." I sat up with a start. "What happened to the girls and the vamps? Did you get them?"

"No, they got away. How many of them did you kill?" Rico sure knew how to wake a girl up.

"Wow, no 'Hi, how are you?' Just straight to the punch, huh?" I needed caffeine if I was going to have this discussion again.

"Here, your favorite coffee." Damien put a grande cup of coffee from Lola's on the table in front of me.

I sniffed the tantalizing aroma. "Mmm, you are an angel. Thank you Damien."

"It was Rico's idea. How many spells did you use? We saw evidence of quite a few."

"Um, my charm bracelet worked quite well at expelling fangs from my body. Then I think I used four or five more? It's all kinda fuzzy right now. You can count the spells in my bag and see what's missing. I took one of each." I lifted my bag up to the table.

"I see you didn't use the red one, that's good. When I noticed you had used spells, I feared you might have used the red one and hurt someone." Rico moved around the booth and sat next to me.

"No, I saved it as my Hail Mary move. It was too cramped in the hallway of that building to use a bomb. The force field was awesome! I want more of those. Too bad it only lasts for one minute. I almost made it out when I threw it at them. There was another vamp who practically ghosted to the exit and blocked my escape. Eventually, I got him outside, and he went up in smoke." At least, I killed one of them.

"Jenna, while I am eternally grateful you made it out in one piece, why were you there to begin with?" I could tell Rico was frustrated. He was breathing out of his mouth and kept running a hand through his hair. It was one of his ways to try and calm himself.

"Rico, I did need some storage space for the store." He didn't need to know I used it as an excuse to check off one more place on the search grid.

"Why did you take so many spells with you if you just wanted to check out some storage space?" He had a point.

"After my last experience, just doing an errand, I decided to be prepared."

"It wasn't the closest storage place to your store. Why did you choose this one?"

"Okay, so I thought I would kill two birds with one stone. I thought using a second story of a storage facility would be a smart way to hide and wait out the storm. The guy with the zodiac boat and beer inspired it." It was the truth.

"Why Castle Storage? Was it the first one you checked out?" Now Damien was interrogating me?

"I used a map of storage places and cross referenced it with cemeteries. This was the closest one to a graveyard. Plus, the name kinda spoke to me." I should have known I'd get busted.

"I have to say, I didn't think it would be dangerous. I had no clue their acolyte was helping them to snatch women." At least, he got what was coming to him.

"What? They're letting acolytes lure women in to them?" Rico was fuming. His nostrils flared, and he slammed a fist down on the table causing my drink to rumble around.

"Don't worry, they killed him for his efforts right in front of me. They had told him to stop bringing them women. Also, the vamps knew who I was and how I'm connected to you. They were worried about getting you involved." They should have just let me go to start with.

"Too late. They are all going down! I can't believe an acolyte actually lured women to their death." Rico and his pack wouldn't stop until this band got what's coming to them, I knew it.

"I think he did it in order to become a vampire. He was trying to prove his worth. Either way, he got the death coming to him, just not the one he wanted." I yawned and took a sip of my piping hot café au lait.

"Why am I so tired? I've fought vamps before and didn't

feel this awful." My body ached, and I really could use more sleep.

"It's all of the magic you used. Because you aren't a witch, those spells took power from you. Your body needs to recover. Let this be a lesson, don't use more than 3 spells. Unless, of course, your life is in danger like today." How much did Rico know about using magic?

"Do you use spells? Have you experienced this before?"

"I have only been given a few spells to use, besides my protection amulet. The protection amulet doesn't take anything from me. The witch who created it gave up some of his power to make the charm work. Which is why they are so rare and expensive." Rico touched the amulet hanging just under his tight black t-shirt.

"What about other spells, Rico? Have you used any of them?"

"Only a handful. I once fought alongside the council when a group of werewolves had made their way to town. The lead witch on the hunt gave me a few red charms along with the brown and pink ones. I'm with you, I like the force field charms the best. Once the fight was over, and we had destroyed the weres, I had to give them back any remaining charms in my possession. Too bad. I used one red stone, and it packs a punch." Rico's eyes were glazed over as he recalled the event.

"You were smart to hold off on using it when you were inside the building. It most likely would have collapsed all around you." It was very odd Rico had to give back the charms, and we are allowed to use them.

"I did need extra rest and food after the battle. As a paranormal creature, my magical aura helped to sustain me and the charms I used. Since you are a human, it takes more out of you. Please remember this." He squeezed my hand, and my heart fluttered.

Darn it! Why did I have to respond to his touch like this. One of these days I'm going to break down and kiss him. Then our protection will be gone. I have to get him out of my system.

I pulled my hand back and made it look like I was just taking a sip of my coffee. "I think I should go home and sleep some more. Will you and the pack keep looking for the girls?"

"Yes. I'll walk you home, and then I'm going back out to search again." Rico scooted out of the booth, and I followed.

"Once I'm rested, I want to join you in the search. You said I could. I think I've proven I can take care of myself now I have the magical charms and amulet." I really didn't understand my desire to go back out and fight vamps again.

I was almost killed earlier, and the after-effects from using magic are worse than any hangover I've ever experienced.

Do I have a hero complex or something?

"We'll see. I don't want you to push it. Using too much magic too soon could seriously hurt you." I let Rico walk me home, but we weren't done with this conversation. Not by a longshot.

My sisters were even worse.

"Jenna! Thank the good Lord! What were you thinking? Going after vampires on your own? What a stupid thing to do!" Kat could be a bit overprotective at times.

"Kat, it was daylight. How was I to know an acolyte worked at the storage facility? If he wasn't trying to impress the vamps, I never would have been in any danger. Besides, I'm safe. The magic worked." All I wanted to do was take a bath and go to bed. Maybe for a couple of days.

"I'm just glad you're home. Promise, no more going out looking for trouble by yourself?" Sam grabbed me and hugged me tightly.

"I promise. You gotta know, I really thought it was safe to go during the daylight. I just wanted to see if my idea was a good one. Turned out, I was right on." I shrugged.

What could I say? It was a dumb move. One I wasn't going to do again.

"Look, I'm exhausted from using so much magic. I'm going to take a hot bath and then go to bed. Rico can explain the side effects of using magic for mundanes." I didn't even wait for anyone to say anything.

After grabbing my pajamas from my dresser, I headed to the bathroom where I set up a relaxing bath with a jasmine bath bomb.

23

JENNA

"*M*mm." I stretched my arms above my head and rolled over in bed. It was dark out.

"I must have slept the entire day away." My stomach gurgled, letting me know I also skipped eating all day.

When I went out to the living room, all was quiet. The living areas were void of life. *Strange.*

Everyone was in bed. They must have been, I realized when I looked at the clock on the microwave. It said 3:24 am.

"Huh, I slept for about twelve hours. After sleeping three hours at Jimmie's. Guess that means I really did use too much magic." It was strange talking to myself but even stranger having no one to chat with.

With a house full of women, there was always someone up to talk to.

There was a note on the kitchen table with an iPhone 7 on a charger. "Jenna, here's a new phone. Same number. This time don't lose your phone during a battle. I got you one of those hard case protectors as well. Please use it." Rico bought me a new phone.

Next to the new phone was a purple, hardcover case.

The type you could use underwater or drop twenty stories, and it would survive. Clunky, but for me, it was perfect.

There was a text message on the phone for me. "*I hope you slept well. Please text me when you wake up, just to let me know you are alright. Rico.*"

I texted back, "*Rico, thank you so much for the new phone! I'll pay you back. I'm fine. Slept soundly & raring to go.*"

Within a minute the phone beeped.

"*Stay home tonight. Tomorrow you can join us. We're almost done. Found nothing. Will speak with vamp queen tomorrow.*"

It was too bad Rico and his pack didn't find anything, but it meant I had a chance to help out.

"Hey, how are you feeling?" Kat schlepped into the kitchen rubbing her eyes and yawning.

I jumped when I heard someone behind me. "Kat! You startled me. Why aren't you asleep?"

"I heard something, so I got up to investigate. Guess it was you. I see you found your new phone. Rico really is good to you." Kat reached into the fridge and pulled out a container of orange juice.

"He's good to us all, and yes, he's especially good to me." I sighed.

"Why aren't you two together?"

"You know why, Kat. Even you said it was wrong."

"I never said it was wrong, just bad timing. I know you, Jenna. If you think it's going to go down badly, it will. Once you believe in yourself and Rico, I will totally support you. Until then, you will be ruining the best thing to ever happen to you."

"Kat, that's not fair."

"It's the truth and deep down you know this. Think about it. If a customer came to you about a guy she liked, but was afraid because she always messed things up. what would you say to her before selling her something?"

I scratched my head. Kat had a point. "Probably something similar to what you just said, and then I would most likely sell her over $100 worth of potions."

"Potions which would work because she believed in them. The power of positive thinking is crazy. The reverse is true, too. If you believe it's going to fail, it will. Plain and simple." Gah! Why was Kat always right?

"You're right. I'll try to work on this."

"You'll stay away from Rico, romantically, until you believe it could work?" Sometimes, Kat felt more like a mother than a sister.

"Yes, Mom. Until the right time, he's just a friend and protector." I put a chocolate pop-tart in the toaster and pushed the lever down. It wasn't the best choice, but if I was going back to bed, this was all I needed until morning. It was a good thing Indie didn't know about our stash of processed foods.

I almost forgot about Rico.

"*Hey, Kat just walked in. I'm gonna eat something and go back to sleep, if possible. Chat tomorrow.*" I put my phone away, after the message sent.

"What did I miss while I was out to the world?"

"Indie and Joseph came back with a van full of stuff. Most went to the pack, but we now have a fully stocked pantry. Nothing much else." Kat sat at the table and sipped her juice.

The toaster popped my pastries into the air, and I grabbed them.

"What about them? Do you think they should wait to start dating?" I didn't think they should wait. They were the perfect couple.

"I'm not interfering with them. You know how Indie is. She's going to make a Joseph doll in case they break up. She's not as bad as you are, but she does do some really psychotic stuff once in a while. I don't want her messing with Joseph."

"Who's messing with Joseph?" Indie walked into the room wearing her tank top and cotton shorts she loved to sleep in.

Oh shoot! Indie wasn't supposed to see my processed toaster pastry!

"Speak of the devil. I was asking if you and Joseph had hooked up yet." I took a bite of my chocolate toaster pastry. A small amount of hot chocolate oozed out of the pastry and landed on my chin.

Indie looked at me and pointed to my chin. "You got something on your face. Looks like enriched flour, dextrose, high fructose corn syrup, and a plethora of other deadly chemicals."

"Yummy." I licked my chin but couldn't get the chocolate off. In the end, I needed a napkin to clean it up.

"Chill, Indie. You were the one who decided we needed to go all organic. You didn't even give us a say in the matter. For the most part, we have changed our diet. Stop bugging me whenever I eat something you wouldn't approve of." It's not like I ate processed food all of the time, just when I was stressed or didn't have time to prepare something healthy.

"So, what about you and Joseph?" I wasn't going to let Indie change the topic.

"We. Well, we had fun yesterday. That's all I'm going to say right now." Indie wasn't going to get away with this secret.

"You stinker! Come on, spill. Is he a good kisser?" Kat and I both broke out laughing.

"I don't kiss and tell." Indie's red cheeks gave her away.

"Oh! You did kiss! Come on, how was it?" Kat asked.

"Stop! Leave me alone. You know better than to jinx things with guys. Leave it alone. When there is anything to share, I will." Indie crossed her arms over her chest.

"Hey! What's going on? A family meeting? Someone forgot to tell me." Sam pursed her lips and walked into the kitchen. "Where's the coffee?"

"Sam, it's too early for coffee. Sorry we woke you up. Kat and I were just teasing Indie about Joseph. They kissed yesterday, but she won't spill the beans."

"Is that all? Of course, they kissed. It was just the two of them all day long. I heard him confirm their date for tomorrow night before he left. I'd say they're an official couple now." Sam had eavesdropped? Sneaky!

"I knew I loved you most, Sam. Thanks for spying on them and getting the details!" I loved it when one of my sisters spied on the other, just as long as they weren't spying on me.

"Joseph got a call from his witch friend later in the day. He's going to restock us with more charms and spells tomorrow. He was really impressed with how well you did against so many vamps, Jenna."

"Indie, stop trying to change the subject. I'm glad we are getting more charms, but you gotta tell us something. When is your date? Where are you going?" She better tell me what's going on.

"Tell us about the date, or I'll turn you into a toad!" That should get her talking. I would do it too. If I had a spell to change her, that is.

"Jenna, you can't change me into a toad! You're so silly! You can only use premade spells from witches. Why would they give you something to change me into a toad?" Indie could be so gullible at times. I loved her.

Laughing, I said, "I can't change you into a toad. I could knock you out, though. Do you want to tell me everything you know? Remember, we are sisters." Surely she would be loyal enough to tell me everything, right?

"Fine, but there isn't much to tell." Indie huffed. "Yesterday was really nice. We got to know each other a lot better. Spending a day just the two of us was perfect. I hope we can spend some more alone time together, but with all of you and his pack, I doubt we get much time together."

"You're probably right. I guess you should find a way to get out of town for a day again." Sam had a great idea.

"Yeah, I second what Sam said."

"I'm staying out of this." Kat was going back to not getting involved. "Do what you want, just be careful and not hurt Joseph. He's a great guy. The kind you could settle down with, once you're ready."

"Are we all going back to bed? Or staying up?" I asked as I ate my chocolate pastry.

"What I want to know is what's going on with you and Ivan, Kat?" Indie might just be in trouble for bringing up Ivan. Last time, Kat was a wee bit defensive.

"Look, we can't be together. So stop bringing it up." Kat stormed off to her room.

"Ouch, looks like we hit a nerve. Do you know why they can't be together?" I personally had no problem with her dating a vampire, as long as he was good to her and us. So far, Ivan had been really nice and helpful.

"Um, no idea." Sam shrugged.

"Maybe, he's just not that into her?" I doubted Indie was right.

"No, I've seen them together. I don't know if love is the

right word, but they are both majorly into each other." Something had to be going on. I'd just have to try and get it out of her, when she wasn't so cranky.

"So what now? Sleep?" Sam asked as she yawned.

"You should go back to sleep. I think I've had enough. How are we doing on inventory? I could make up some more voodoo dolls until everyone is ready to get up." Too bad it was so early and dark.

Spending some time reading at Lola's Coffee Shop would be a great way to spend my morning. I couldn't remember the last time I had done so. Before meeting Rico and learning all about the paranormal world, I used to spend one morning a week there. I missed the simpler times.

"We're running low on a few supplies, but you should be able to spend an hour or two making more dolls. I'll do a run today and pick up more supplies."

"Indie, you should get Joseph to go with you. A big, strong guy like him would be perfect on a supply run." I winked at Indie, hoping she'd get the hint.

"Just don't make a voodoo doll of him, no matter what!" Sam was a bit late in her request.

I had already asked Indie to forego the usual with Joseph. Indie said she wouldn't make a doll of him. I guess I'll just have to wait and see if she sticks to her word.

24

JENNA

"*R*ico, what are you doing here so early?" It wasn't even nine o'clock yet when someone knocked on my door.

My sisters were still getting ready for the day. I was actually getting ready to leave and head to Lola's to get in some reading and fantastic coffee.

"I had to come to town to meet with the vampire queen. Before heading over, I wanted to see how you're doing and bring you some coffee." He handed me a drink carrier with disposable coffee mugs from Lola's.

"Ahhh, you are awesome! Thank you. I was just headed there myself. Come on in." I waved at Rico to enter.

"She had a few fresh beignets as well." Rico waved a small paper bag in front of my face and the aroma of cinnamon and fresh pastry was to die for.

"OH, you are on a roll! First a new phone, now my favorite breakfast. What's next? A Porsche?" I laughed.

"When's your birthday?" Rico winked and headed to the kitchen.

"I think I'd have to marry you if you got me a Porsche for my birthday." Okay, that was awkward.

Why did I say that out loud?

Rico cleared this throat and whispered, "I'd be good with that."

I took a café au lait from the drink carrier and looked away from him. He couldn't have intended for me to hear his mad rumbling. Sometimes I say the stupidest things.

"So, what's on your calendar for today? You know, after you see the queen."

"I was thinking I could take you to lunch and maybe just get to know each other better. Since we met, it's been all about vampires and witches. I would like to get to know you without all of the vampire drama. Then I want to kick your butt on the mat." His cheese-eating grin totally made the tension in the room disappear.

"You want to take me to lunch and then beat me up? Nice, really nice, Rico." I couldn't help but laugh.

It was accurate. If we sparred, he would kick my butt. I had yet to best him in a match. Sure, I have gotten in a few good punches but nothing good enough to win.

"You make it sound so awful. How about lunch and a work out?" Rico could be funny, sometimes.

"Ok, sounds good to me. Let me know when you're done with the queen." I'm just glad I didn't have to accompany him there. Hanging out with vampires was the last thing I wanted. Then I'd have to take another rubbing alcohol shower. No thanks.

*O*nce Rico was done, he called, and we met downstairs in the shop. I wanted all of the girls to hear how things went with the queen.

"So, what did the high and mighty queen of blood have to say?" Kat seemed to have an extra amount of hatred for the queen. Could it have something to do with Ivan?

"I told her about the vampires Jenna fought and how they did have the storm girls in their possession. Of course, Celeste said she knew of no vampires who were breaking the laws. She promised to begin her own investigation immediately." Rico rolled his eyes.

"I take it you don't believe her?" The eye rolling is what tipped me off.

"No, I don't. I'm sure she didn't condone the actions of those vampires, but I do think she knows more than what she told me. I just hope I find them before she does."

"Why?" I asked.

"If she finds the missing girls, and they are in the hands of any of her vampires, I would bet she'd kill them so no one could say who took them. Since Jenna has seen the vamps, the queen would just keep her vamps locked up, or she might stake them herself. Just depends on who they are. I don't think the girls would survive the queen."

"Oh, then what are we waiting for? Forget the lunch and work-out, let's get back out there and start searching again." This was much more important than quality alone time with Rico.

Besides, I didn't know how I felt about being alone with him on a date. He didn't say it was a date, but since it would have been just the two of us, it would have felt like a date.

"My pack is already out there. Are you sure you want to search for the girls instead of more training?"

"Rico, are you trying to keep me out of the field? Was today all about keeping me from searching for those girls?" He better not be doing this, or I would flip my lid.

"Of course not. I was just being selfish. We don't get much alone time. When Indie and Joseph went to Price Club the other day, they got to know each other a lot better." He wouldn't look me in the eye.

"Is that it? You really don't have a problem with me going into the field?" Something felt off, and I had a feeling he wasn't being honest with me.

He fidgeted with his hands and stayed silent.

"Rico, which is it? You wanted a date during this mess, or you wanted to keep me out of the field? Don't lie to me." I narrowed my eyes and pursed my lips, while I waited for his response.

"A bit of both, really."

"How dare you! You know this is important to me. I want to help those girls, and after everything I've been through, I need to help even more!" I slapped his shoulder. Which only hurt me and not him.

"Stupid wolf-shifter!" I stormed to my room to change my clothes.

I yelled out, "Kat! Do you want to go on patrol with me? Maybe we can get Joseph or Damien to join us. I know one wolf who WON'T be joining us today!" Rico could kiss my butt if he thought I'd spend time with him now.

"Sure, I need to change and load up on charms. Sam, can I use your messenger bag?" Kat went to her room to change.

"Wait, you can't go without me. I'm sorry, but Jenna you need to rest another day before using magic." Rico wasn't going to get away with trying to manipulate me.

"Screw you, Rico! I don't appreciate men trying to

manipulate me. Turns out you're no better than any of the other guys I've met over the years!" Stupid men. All they ever wanted was to control women. Not this woman, not again.

"Alpha men may be hot in books and movies, but not in real life!" Who did he think I was? Some waif who needed rescuing from herself?

When I came out into the living room, dressed in tight black pants, a black cotton t-shirt, jean jacket, and my knee-high Doc Martens' boots, Rico's jaw dropped. I knew I looked hot, and he could forget about hanging with me today.

"Close your mouth, Rico. You don't want flies getting in." I smirked.

"Jenna, you can't wear that outfit." Rico sputtered.

"Oh, I can, and I am. It's quite comfortable. These boots are perfect for kicking butt. Today, I want to kick someone's backside." I would have preferred kicking his, but he would probably catch my foot before it hit its target.

Kat came out dressed like me. We were going to attract vampire attention, I hoped. If they came after us, we would kill them and any of their acolytes who got in the way. Although, I wasn't sure how many they had left now. It looked like they only had two males left to assist them. They would need to recruit again, unless they were acting with the vampire queen's approval.

"Let's go. We can call Damien while we head out and see where he is." I pulled my new cell phone out of my jean jacket's inner pocket and dialed Damien.

"Jenna, good to hear from you. Are you with Rico?"

"Yes, but I want to meet up with you guys and patrol. Kat and I have a bunch of spells and are ready to kick some blood-sucker butts!" I slammed the door behind me and Kat when we walked out.

"Why aren't you patrolling with Rico?"

"He's an idiot and a misogynist pig. Kat and I are patrolling. Either you tell me where you are, or we go on our own." I'm not sure Kat would agree to that, but Damien didn't know any better.

"Okay, I want to hear this story. How about we meet you at the taco shop in the Magnolia Shopping Center? My guys are hungry. Then we can get back out and keep searching." Damien better not be trying to stall.

"Alright, we'll see you there soon. Thanks, Damien." I put my phone back in my pocket as Kat and I took off in the van. Magnolia Mall was too far to walk and public transit would take too long.

"Do you think he'll follow us?" Kat pulled out of our alley and headed to the mall.

"Probably. I'm sure he's on the phone now with Damien to see where we will be." I looked out the window and tried to calm myself down.

"I hate when men try to control me. I went up against five vampires and an acolyte, and I walked away after killing a vamp. How dare he think I couldn't handle this!"

Everyone wonders why I haven't had good luck with men, this is exactly why. Just when I start to lower my walls, they go and screw it all up.

"Jenna, I know it wasn't cool. However, I think he was just trying to look out for you. He went about it all wrong, but I think he had your best interests at heart." I couldn't believe Kat was defending him.

"Phft. Really? You're taking his side?"

"No, I'm always on your side, Jenna. You're my sister. Just

give Rico a break. He is an alpha wolf. I bet his emotions are much more volatile than ours are once a month."

"That doesn't give him the right to try and control me. If he didn't want me out looking, he could have talked to me about it."

"You're right, but something tells me he isn't used to having to discuss things with people. I bet the wolves just listen to him when he tells them what to do. When he asks you to do things, you aren't very good at listening."

"That's because I'm a strong, independent woman who can look out for herself. I don't need someone dictating my actions for me. How would you feel if he did this to you?" I crossed my arms over my chest and turned my head to watch Kat's reaction.

"I would have punched him."

"Exactly my point, Kat."

"But Jenna, I'm not falling for him. You are. If you want to have a relationship with him, you're going to have to listen to his worries. Letting him protect you will be your job as his girlfriend."

"WHAT!? I can't believe you, of all people, are suggesting I play the weak, little girl card to get a guy." I was never going to be that girl. I couldn't believe Kat even suggested it.

"Jenna, it's all part of the game. You have to let the guy think he's protecting you. Especially with an alpha wolf. It's something genetic. He can't help but feel the need to keep you safe. It probably has something to do with animal instincts. The need to protect a mate is very strong in the animal kingdom."

"What about black widows?" I tried very hard to stifle a laugh. Black widows mated and then killed the males.

"Or the praying mantis? She bites his head off." Kat started laughing and the tension between us faded.

"Do you really think a woman has to play weak in order to keep a guy? Kat, this isn't you."

"Jenna, I don't think you have to do it with all men. Just alpha men, like Rico. They are wired differently. I watched you two. There are times when you enjoy how he takes care of you. You do like a take charge guy, as long as he doesn't take it too far." Kat the psychologist.

"When did you get so smart? How do you know about alpha men?" My shoulders relaxed, and I watched as the NOLA scenery flew by. We were getting closer to the mall.

"I've known Ivan awhile now. When we first met, we did try the whole dating thing. It didn't work out but not because he's an alpha male." Kat bit her lower lip and stared straight ahead.

"Kat, can you tell me what happened?"

"Now isn't the right time for this conversation. Just know I did try making it work and for a while it did. I played the doting girlfriend who let her big, bad monster of a boyfriend take care of her. If he wasn't a vampire, it probably would have worked."

"I'll let you keep your secret for now. When this is over, I want the whole story. You've never kept secrets like this before. I understand keeping the truth away from us when you did but not now. We need to know why it couldn't work with Ivan when the two of you seem so in love."

Kat pounded the steering wheel. "Fine. When the girls are all safe, I will tell you."

"Thanks, Kat." I stayed quiet for the rest of the ride. Kat seemed like she needed the peace and quiet after our conversation.

25

JENNA

"*L*adies, you look like you're dressed to kill." Damien looked us both up and down and let his gaze linger a bit longer on Kat.

"Thanks, and yes, we are." Kat winked at him and walked past.

"Where are we headed today? Don't you dare pull a Rico and try to keep us out of the fight either. The best way for us to learn and improve is to be in the field with you guys. You can't keep us from getting attacked forever. We just seem to be vampire magnets." I really hoped Damien would be smarter than his idiot alpha.

"Jenna's right. We do seem to attract vampire attention, even when just going out for Chinese take-out. You're better off training us, so we can defend against any attack." This was the aggressive Kat. The one you didn't want to go up against.

Damien put his hands in the air. "Fine, I'll be sure to take you to places we suspect vampire activity. Just don't cry when you get attacked. Oh, don't kill the humans, either.

They may have made some bad choices, but Rico never kills them."

"What do you do with acolytes who love their roles and don't want out?" I did wonder what happened when they came across these kind of people. Did they just send them back to the vampire queen?

"We send them off to a rehab facility. Being an acolyte is an addiction, just like drugs or alcohol. There are a couple of facilities run by psychologists who know the truth. When we capture an acolyte, we send them for help." Damien motioned for his men to get up and join us.

"Do they ever rejoin society? Or do they run back to the vampires?" I had seen how devoted acolytes can be. I couldn't imagine rehab working for them.

"Since Rico started sending them away a few years back, we have only seen about fifteen percent return to their old acolyte lives. The rest are grateful and integrate back into society. Some even become vampire hunters." Why couldn't Rico talk to me the same way Damien does? Damien treats us like equals, not little girls who need protection.

"Damien, thank you for telling us this and for treating us like adults instead of cutesy dolls who need a man to protect them." Too bad Damien wasn't the alpha, Rico would probably be much easier to manage.

"Rico really stepped in it, didn't he?" Damien directed his question to Kat.

"Yeah. I would have slapped him if he said those things to me. The guy needs to learn to chill and trust Jenna more. She really has improved, and now with magic, we can kick some serious demon butt."

"Alright, there are two rules. I will treat you just like my pack members if you follow these two rules."

"What are they?" I could follow two rules, I hoped.

"One, you listen to what I say. There must be a hierarchy when in battle. All military units function this way. including local police." Damien was someone I could follow into battle. He had proven to be fair and trustworthy. Plus, he didn't treat me like a fragile doll.

"Ok, I can do that. What's the second one?" I stated while Kat nodded her agreement.

"Two, you let Kat use the magic first. I know you used up a lot of magic yesterday. Rico wasn't kidding when he said you needed to recover."

"But..."

"No. You listen to me. This is part of following orders. I have no problem with you using magic, as long as it is done properly."

"What if I need to use a force field spell, and Kat is busy?" Surely, he wouldn't have a cow if it was life or death.

"Only use a spell if there is nothing left to do. Save it as your Hail Mary. Trust me. I have seen humans overdo it with magic. It's not pretty." He was right, of course. Joseph warned us all about overuse of magic.

"I can do it. I won't use magic, unless there are no options left for me." I could do this. There were other ways I could help, like ushering the girls to safety if we found them. Or fighting off any acolytes.

"Thank you, Jenna. If you don't follow my rules, you won't be going on any future patrols. This is very serious. Disregarding orders can not only get you in danger but also the rest of your team. I won't allow you to do anything which could injure or kill anyone on my team. Got it?" Now Damien was starting to sound like a drill sergeant, or at least what I assumed one sounded like.

"Got it." I almost saluted and said, *aye, aye, captain*.

Something told me my snarky attitude wouldn't be appreci-
ated at the moment.

For Damien, and Rico, to take me seriously, I had to
behave properly. I've seen enough to know this isn't a joking
matter. While I was still ticked off with Rico, Damien had a
few good points. I needed to follow orders, something I was
never good at.

Outside of my sisters, I had never been much of a team
player. This situation called for something different than my
normal style. It was time for me to join the team and help
where I could, not just do what I wanted to do.

"Damien, I really do want to help. So just tell me what to
do, and I promise to do my best." Giving it my best was
really all anyone could ask of me.

"Thank you, Jenna. We should check the attic of the
mall. Sometimes, vamps will set up temporary nests here.
It's a great place to hide. At night, once everyone has left,
they can steal all they want from the shops, if they are in the
corridors."

"Luke, why don't you join me and the girls? Jose, you
split off with the rest of the pack and search for signs of
blood-sucker activity. We'll take the attics." Damien led Kat
and I to the entrance of the area marked "Employees Only."

"What's back here?" I had never worked in a mall so I
never had access to these areas.

"Mostly just the back entrances to each store. There's a
hallway going from one end of the mall to the other. This is
how they take out trash during the day and receive deliv-
eries as well. The doors are usually locked tight. So let me
know if you see a door wedged open or looks to have been
forced open." Damien opened the access door and held it
for both Kat and I. All of the men in this pack were gentleman, for the most part.

I heard Damien answer his phone. It sounded like he was talking to Rico. I didn't want to eavesdrop, but I did.

Sounded like Rico wanted to join us. I really hoped he didn't.

Did being a gentlemen go hand in hand with being a misogynist? Or was it just my bad luck to meet gentlemen who had no belief in women's abilities?

I don't hate men. Actually, I love them. So why is it I have had such bad luck in the romance department? Something to ponder another time, I suppose. Now, it was time to focus on the mission and pay attention to details.

We turned left and headed to the far end of the mall. As we went along, I read the signs on the doors. My credit card itched to come out and shop when we walked past Vicky's Closet. They had the best pajama sets.

I continued to scan the doors and stopped in front of one with no sign. "Damien, look at the lock on this door. I can't tell if it's been broken into, but it looks to be an empty store. The deadbolt has been scratched a few times where it locks into the jamb."

Damien turned around and came back to where I stood. "Good eye, Jenna. Stand back." Damien wiggled the door handle, and it opened.

Kat and I took several steps back and let Damien and Luke go first.

Inside was black as night. The only light shone in from the hallway we were standing in.

Once the guys were inside, I stuck my head in and looked around. "Kat, do you have a penlight? I can't see much."

Without saying a word, Kat handed me a small flashlight which looked more like a black ballpoint pen than a flashlight. After I clicked it on, I flashed a small amount of light over the floor. There were stacks of boxes surrounded by discarded paper and trash. Even some Chinese take-out boxes were strewn on the ground.

I whispered, "Damien, someone's living here. That take-out box is fresh. There aren't even any bugs hanging out yet."

He turned around and put a finger to his lips. Of course, he knew it already. If someone was inside, he could probably hear them. A wolf could pick up on a heartbeat at least twenty feet away.

Vamps didn't have heartbeats, but storm girls and acolytes did.

26

RICO

"*W*hen am I ever going to learn?" I knew pushing Jenna away from the case was wrong. She's too strong-willed for her own good. I just didn't think it would push her away from me or make her so mad she would go out to patrol without me by her side.

Women. Can't live with them and can't live without them. How do couples last so long?

"Damien, I ticked off Jenna like you wouldn't believe." I dialed my second in command hoping he was going to work with Jenna, and protect her.

"I know. She and Kat are here with me now. Don't worry, I'll watch over her and protect them both." Damien was the next best wolf to protect my Jenna. She would be safe with him.

"How do you suppose I make this up to her? She compared me to all of her idiot ex-boyfriends. I always thought I was a better man than most. Am I really that bad?" I couldn't be so awful, could I?

"You are a fantastic Alpha, Rico. I think with Jenna, you just need to dial back the Alpha role. She's a very modern, independent woman. From the sounds of things, she's had bad luck with guys trying to control her. I know you don't want to control her, but maybe you can come off as a control-freak to a human who doesn't get the whole alpha role?" I hadn't thought of it in those terms. Damien made a good point.

"Alright, I'll try to let her make more of her own decisions. I just don't know how my wolf will handle letting her walk into a dangerous situation." This was the crux of the problem. My wolf.

He sees Jenna as our mate. It's the male's job to protect the female. I know all about women's lib, and I support it. There are several females in my pack who could kick some serious butt. Some of them would best all of the men, except for Damien and me. There's a reason why I'm the alpha, and Damien is the beta. We have proven ourselves to be the strongest in the pack.

A wolf pack hierarchy is based on strength. He, or she, who is the toughest gets the leadership roles. The only reason Joseph is regarded so highly is because he has the magical connections, and he saved my pack many times using his knowledge of alchemy. Otherwise, he would be the lowest of the low in the omega group.

Omega's are the bottom of the pack. They do the jobs no one else wants to do, kind of like a grunt in the military. Some packs treat their omegas like dirt, but I don't. Sure, they get the grunt jobs, but they aren't beat up like in some other packs.

Dialing back my wolf when it comes to Jenna is going to be very tough.

"Hey, do you mind if I come by the mall and check on Jenna? Do you think she would hate me more if I did so?" I wasn't going to tell her what to do, I just wanted to be around in case she needed me.

"I wouldn't, if I were you. If you do, just hang back. Don't join our team. Maybe you could lead the other team? Or take some of the pack from Jose's team and check out somewhere else? It could keep you close by, but not too close to make her feel watched." Damien was smart. I knew there was a reason I confided in him.

"Right. I'll call Jose and meet up with them. Thanks Damien." I hung up and dialed Jose. If Damien ever left us, Jose would be in line for the Beta role.

"Hey, boss. What's up?" Jose answered on the second ring.

"I'm heading your way. Wondered if you had some men who wanted to join me in searching the area around the mall." I really wanted to be closer to Jenna.

"Did you want to take over my team? I'm cool if you want to lead." Jose never seemed to mind when I took over. He knew his position in the pack well.

"Nah, you can keep leading, I just wanted a few wolves to help me search nearby. I don't want to be at the mall, unless you need me." Not really the truth, but it was reality.

"Sure thing. Call me when you get here. I'm heading to the south side of the mall. Damien and his crew are going to search the attic."

"See you soon." I was about to hang up when something in Jose's voice changed.

"Boss, don't hang up. You better hurry and get here. Something's going on. I see people running from where Damien's team should be right now."

"Jose, go back them up. I'll be there as soon as I can." I hung up, jumped in my car, and sped to the mall. There was no way speed limits would get in my way of protecting Jenna.

I dialed Damien, but it went to voicemail after four rings. It meant he was busy, probably fighting vampires. Then I tried Jenna. No answer on her phone either. Surely she would have answered me if she could, right?

Kat was next on my list to call. If she didn't answer, then I knew they were in danger.

"Son of a biscuit eater!" Kat didn't answer either.

27

JENNA

"*J*enna, so good of you to come and bring your friend. We could use some more fresh blood."

Oh stink! I recognized the voice. It was Alexy from the storage facility.

"I don't think you're going to like my friends. They tend to kill vampires in very gruesome ways." Now I wished Rico was here.

"The wolves aren't welcome, I meant Kat. Yes, I know all of your bandmates. Scott may not have been the smartest acolyte, but he was right when he said we were all fans of your music. If you would just agree to serve me, you and your sisters would live. I would take very good care of you." Alexy was delusional if he thought we would become acolytes.

"Sorry, the wolves have a much better health plan. I think I'll stick with them." The wolves would do everything they could to keep us alive, I doubted the vamps would keep us alive for very long, even if we volunteered.

"Oh, don't be like that. We can give you immortality. What can the wolves offer? Furry kisses? Obedience?

Wouldn't you rather play your music for eternity?" His voice kept moving around, almost like he was flying above us.

I turned to where I heard his voice last and didn't see anything. In fact, I didn't even see the wolves anymore. They had disappeared while I was chatting up the vamp.

"Kat, where'd the guys go?" I whispered in her ear.

She looked around with wide eyes and shrugged. They must have moved super fast, just like the vamps.

"Get some spells out. We're gonna need them," I whispered again.

Kat reached into her bag and pulled out a few of the different colored stones. She put the red ones back. Again, we weren't in a place where throwing bombs would work well. Maybe in open spaces, like a park, we could use them safely. Well, as safely as you can use a magical bomb.

I picked out two pink charms and two yellow ones. Those worked the best when I fought the vamps yesterday. Kat shook her head, so I put them in my pocket to show I was only going to hold them for in case of an emergency. She nodded in understanding.

She also picked up a few each of the pink and yellow ones. Kat even pulled out two blue stones, then she put the rest back in her bag. I never did get around to using a blue one. I hoped she opened with it when the vamps were close enough.

I jerked my head to the left when I heard boxes falling. With the penlight, I tried to see what was going on. Whatever, or whoever, knocked over the boxes was too far away for my little penlight to see. At best, we could make out the outlines of boxes up to five feet away.

"Jenna, the door." Kat pointed to the door we came through, and we tried to make our way back to it. If we could get the door opened, we might have more light to see.

"Uh, uh, uh. No leaving now that the party is just starting. You two are the special guests." Alexy was toying with us.

He stayed in the shadows so we couldn't see him. Smart. It would make throwing spells at him harder.

"Alexy, we just wanted to get some light on the party. Unlike paranormals, we can't see well in the dark. Who wants to party when they can't see everyone?" I continued to make my way to the door.

Hands grabbed me from behind and fangs tried to grab onto my neck. The protection charm warmed my wrist and covered my body in a warm glow. Alexy was thrown back against the wall with a thud.

Since I knew where the sound was coming from, I turned my pen light toward Alexy. His face was set in a scowl, and he tried shaking the effects of the electrical discharge off before getting up.

"Now, Kat. Blue," I hoped she heard me whisper.

Kat pulled out the blue spell stone and threw it at Alexy's chest. He put his hand out to grab the spell.

"Ow!" Alexy screamed as the stone blew a hole in his hand and landed in his ribcage.

It wasn't a death blow, but it had to hurt like a knife or steak to the chest would.

I could see the hole in his hand. His disbelief was evident on his face as he looked between his hand and his chest.

This was my chance to end him. I pulled a stake from my backpack and ran at him with Kat on my heels.

Alexy must have been too stunned to pay any attention until I was right in front of him. I dropped to my knees and slammed the stake in his chest, next to the spell stone.

The vampire's eyes turned red with rage, and he grabbed

my wrist and pulled it back from his body. I left the stake in his chest, and he laughed.

"Oh, that hurts. Jenna, why would you try to hurt me after all we've been through?" Alexy used his other hand to pull out the stake.

For some reason I was too weak to drive it far enough into his chest. Was this why I shouldn't be out so soon after using too much magic? Was my physical strength zapped away?

Kat was directly behind me and holding her own stake. She lunged at the vamp who moved me directly in front of him. I was now a vampire shield.

"Oh, Kat. You don't want to hurt your sister, do you? She's decided to protect me from you."

"Let her go, and I will willingly give you my neck."

"Kat, NO! You can't do that." What was she thinking?

"I'm not falling for any tricks, girl. I know I can't bite your neck until your protection spell wears off." Alexy stood up and pulled me tight against his body, while wrapping one arm around my middle to keep me in place.

"It's no trick. If I agree to allow you to bite, you can." Kat was nuts.

"Drop your stake and come closer. Why would you want to let me bite you?"

"Because I've been bitten before. I want that euphoria again."

"Kat, what are you doing? Damien will save us as soon as he's done with the other vamps." We could hear some scuffling and sounds of grunts. I guessed our two guys were fighting the other vamps. I hadn't seen or heard anyone else yet.

"Ah, yes. Why weren't you made an acolyte? If you enjoyed the vampire who tasted you, why are you with your sisters?" Alexy was licking his lips next to my ear. The sounds made me cringe and gag.

"Don't do this, Kat. It's not worth it. We can hold out."

"Actually, you can't. If you get in the way, I will just snap your neck. It's a waste of perfectly good blood, but I will do it, if you don't shut up. I want to taste your sister who's willingly giving herself to me. It's so much more enjoyable when a human begs to be drank."

"I don't want to hold out. I dream about the vamp who drank from me over a year ago. This is what I want. He was supposed to come back for me, but he never did." Kat never told me about this.

Was it a ruse? Or did she really feel this way? If it was a ruse, Kat's a great actor.

"Your wolf friends must have killed him. It's alright, you can join my acolytes. Seems we are a bit low at the moment. If you are good enough, I will eventually turn you into an immortal god like myself." Alexy really had issues if he thought he was a god.

Either way, I had to play along with her moves. "Kat, don't do this. You'll lose all of us if you join him."

"Jenna, you have your wolf. I want a vamp. Can't you understand? Human men just don't do it for me. Not since I learned about the paranormal."

I heard a wolf howl, I hoped it meant he killed a vamp and not that he was in trouble. Then several more howls joined in. Jose was near. He was bringing back-ups. How did he know?

Why were Damien and Luke not helping us? They should have left the vamps they were fighting and come to find us. Surely they knew Alexy was with us.

Kat grabbed my shoulder and dropped the stake. She pulled me back from Alexy and bared her neck to him.

Alexy pushed me away from him and grabbed Kat. He pulled her tight against his body and moaned. "I can tell you and I are going to have a lot of fun."

Kat moaned her pleasure in a breathy voice, "Yes, take me. I'm all yours."

I sat there stunned for minute as she really did appear to be enjoying the vampire's arms around her.

Kat was too close to the vamp for me to use any of the spells I had on me. The force field would trap her in it with him. Anything else I used would hurt her, possibly even kill her.

I watched in horror as Alexy's fang elongated, and he slowly moved to her neck. His eyes were on me the entire time. The smile he had on his face was that of a monster. He watched me as I cringed in horror. I think my fear gave him even more enjoyment. Before biting Kat's neck, he licked her veins.

Kat rasped out, "Stop teasing me already. I want this, please."

She ran her arms down the side of the vampire, like she was caressing his body. Then she brought her hands back up. She had something in her right hand. It was too dark to make out.

Right as Alexy went to bite Kat's neck, she moved her hand to his back.

I couldn't watch Alexy bite my sister, but I also couldn't take my eyes off of what was about to happen. His fangs sank into her neck, or they tried. Her protective charm exploded around her and forcefully threw Alexy back against the wall.

Alexy's eyes went wide right before he sunk to the ground.

"OW! Crap, that hurt!" Kat pulled her hand out from behind the vampire and held it gingerly.

"What did you just do?" I shook my head to clear out the horror bouncing around and looked closer at the blood sucker on the ground.

"I pulled a stake out of my boots and positioned it behind his heart. When he tried to bite me, the force of my protective charm blew him against the stake hard enough to penetrate his rib cage and get his heart." She's a genius!

"Wow, you really gambled with that move." Now we needed to get his body outside so the sun would make it go poof.

"Grab his legs, and I'll grab him under his arms. We can carry him out the back. There's a roll-up door just a few feet away. It should lead to a loading dock, I hope."

"Wait, I need to find something to force the door to the walkway to stay open." I looked around for something heavy to hold the door fully open.

"Ah-hah!" There were two heavy boxes not far from the door. I dragged them both closer and opened the door all the way before pushing the boxes against it.

"Let's go. Then we need to find Damien." I walked back to the body and helped Kat pick it up.

When we made our way out to the roll-up door, I heard screaming.

"What's going on?" Kat looked to me and scanned the area.

"I don't see anything. I wonder if the wolves took the fight out the front door of the shop we were in?" Would Damien bring a fight out into the open?

Kat dropped her part of the vamp, so she could open the roll-up door.

"I'm surprised a key isn't needed to open this door." Kat

pulled a lever, and then she pulled a long chain down which rolled the door up.

"We don't need it up high, just enough to roll the body into direct sunlight. Is the sun shining on this side of the building?" I could only see shadows on the ground just past where the door opened up about two feet.

"I'm not sure. I'll open the door a bit more. Look underneath and let me know." Kat pulled on the chain some more and it rolled up further.

I dropped the vamps legs and got down on my hands and knees.

"Ahhh!" I screamed when I saw boots running toward the gate.

"Close it! Someone's coming fast," I screamed.

"Don't close it! It's me, Rico."

"Oh! You scared me, Rico." I put a hand over my beating chest. It was going so fast and hard I thought it might beat right out of my body.

Rico rolled under the door and stood up in a flash. He scowled when he noticed the dead vamp at our feet.

"What happened?" Rico kicked the blood-sucker's body.

"Kat killed him. It was...an odd way of doing it." I wasn't about to tell Rico the details, not until I spoke with Kat further. She took a huge gamble with the protection spell.

"Vampires really are stupid and gullible." Kat smirked.

After I took a deep breath, I said, "We need to get him into the sunlight. Looks like we are on the shadow side of the building."

"Don't worry. I can run him into the light. Stay here, don't move." Rico pointed his finger at me.

"Believe me, I'm not going anywhere until you return. Hurry up, I think Damien and Luke need help." I continued to take calming breaths as Rico rolled the dead vamp under the door and followed it outside.

"Roll the door up a bit more. I want to watch it burn." I sat on the hard concrete floor and watched Rico pick up the body and run faster than any human should.

When he reached the sunlight, Rico threw the bloodsucker into the light. Kat and I both watched as Alexy's hands caught on fire, and then the rest of his body went up in ash.

Rico waved his hand in front of his face as he turned to rush back to us.

"I always hate when the ash gets in my nose and mouth. Remember, throw the body into the light and run away as fast as you can. The ash seems to spread quickly, and it's a pain to get out of your sinuses."

"Thanks for the tip, Rico." Kat rolled the door down and pushed the locking lever back in place once Rico was inside.

28

JENNA

"How did you get separated from Damien? Where is he?" Rico wiped the ash off his face and pulled out a handkerchief. He blew his nose, probably trying to get dead vamp ash out.

"I really don't know where Damien and Luke are. We all entered the back of the store together. It was an empty store, I think. No sign on the door, so we all assumed vacant. It was really dark in their stockroom. Damien and Luke disappeared, and Alexy showed up, taunting us." I led us back to the opened door.

"Alexy caught me when I tried to stab him with my stake. I got the right spot, but for some reason I couldn't muster the strength needed." When we walked through the door, I pulled out my pen light.

There was a decent amount of light shining in from the open door, but the edges of the room were still shrouded in shadows.

"I hate to say I told you so, but...this is exactly why you needed another day of rest. With so much magic use, your body just isn't strong enough, yet." Rico came up next to me and smelled the air.

"I get it now. It's strange, other than being tired, my muscles felt fine. Why wouldn't I be able to tell I had lost some strength?" This magic use business made no sense whatsoever.

"Magic use has a cost. If you are a regular magic user, then you will just lose some of your magical abilities for a short time if you overdo it. For non-magical people, it costs you your strength. Sometimes, you might even lose the ability to walk or see for a short time. So, please, do yourself a favor, and don't overuse magic. Both of you." Rico should have told me this yesterday. I might have listened more if he had.

"Shh." Rico held up his hand and slowly walked forward, further into the store.

"How many vampires were in this coven? You killed two now, right?" Rico was sniffing the air and looking around cautiously.

"I saw a total of five vamps at the storage facility. There should only be three left."

"There are more than three vamp scents here. I'm also picking up on multiple humans. This was a larger coven than we thought." Rico stopped so suddenly I almost walked right into his back.

"What? Do you sense something?" Kat asked from behind me.

"I hear fighting, but it isn't contained in the store front. This must be what caused the scene Jose saw when I was on the phone with him earlier." Rico opened the door from the stockroom to the vacant shop.

"How did it move outside the shop? If this is a vacant store, there would be a fence up in front so you couldn't even see inside." I shopped here enough to know when they had a vacant store, they put a fence covering the store's windows.

"There is always a door leading inside the empty shops, so workers can come and go." Rico looked out into the shop before motioning for us to follow him.

Now I could hear screams coming from the mall and animal growls. Had the pack shifted?

"Stay close to me. I don't want to lose you in the chaos out front. Kat, get some spells ready. Jenna, please don't use any. Rely on your protection charm. It won't steal your strength to power it. The witch who created it used his own personal magic to charge it. Which is why they are so difficult to get, normally." Rico looked back at me and Kat before moving forward into the practically empty store.

I could see light coming in from the open door on the gate outside the shop. The store had been set up with a few couches. There were more boxes were strewn throughout the retail part of the store, and a mini fridge was set-up along the left wall.

No one was inside the store anymore. I couldn't tell how many people or vamps had been here, but it did feel like it could have been more than what I had seen before. There were several piles of clothes thrown up against the right wall. Had to be enough for at least a dozen people.

In the back corner was a cage. The door was open, but I could tell people had been inside of it. Burger wrappers and other types of fast food refuse littered the floor of the metal cage. It was big enough to hold a couple of bears or five storm girls. This must be where they went after the storage place.

"Kat, look." I pointed to the black-barred cage and shivered thinking how horrible it must have been for those girls.

"Son of a biscuit eater!" Rico never used swear words around us. Just one more sign of his being a gentleman.

"What? What did you find?" I approached him and stifled a scream.

Laying in the front, right corner of the store was a human girl. There were multiple bite marks around her neck and shoulders. Her shirt was ripped, obviously to give them more access to her neck. Blood trailed down the front of what was left of her shirt, and she had a vacant expression on her face.

"Is she dead?" She sure looked dead.

Rico knelt down next to her and put his fingers on her neck, checking for a pulse.

"She's alive, but barely. Shoot! I can't leave her here, but we can't take her either." Rico stood up and kicked a hole in the wall next to the girl's body.

"Can Kat and I stay here with her?" I wanted to fight, but if this girl was still alive, we owed it to her.

"No. It's too dangerous to leave you alone. I know you can fight, but the scent of her blood will most likely bring the vamps back. I'll call Joseph and see if he can get over here with his emergency kit." Rico pulled out his phone and called Joseph.

"Kat, is there anything you can do to help her? You've had more first-aid training then the rest of us." I bit my lower lip, trying not to cry, as I looked down at the poor girl dying.

"Unless you have a way for me to give her your blood, there is nothing I can do for her. Well, I could wrap her neck. It might help stop the last of her blood from dropping. At best, it could give her another hour before she died." My sister wiped a lone tear from her cheek before turning around.

Kat walked away from us and looked through the pile of clothes. She brought back a few t-shirts and began to tear them in strips. "Here, help me make some bandages from these shirts. Don't wrap her neck too tightly. I don't want to cut off blood flow, I just want to stop it from leaking out of her wounds."

"Okay." I tried to tear the shirts, but I just didn't have the strength. "Do you have any scissors? I can't seem to tear the shirts."

Kat started a couple of tears on the shirt she was holding. "Here, see if you can finish the tears for me. I'll start the next shirt."

Thankfully, I was able to tear the grey shirt into strips. The shirt had a logo on it for Castle Storage. This was probably one of Scott's old t-shirts. I used what little strength I had and tore it to pieces.

Once the shirt was torn, I took a few of the wider strips and wrapped them around the girl's neck. Blood seeped through the material, so I wrapped another one on just a bit tighter.

"Kat, does this look right?" I pointed to the girl's neck.

The blood flow was already beginning to slow down. The second strip I put around her neck only had a little bit of blood seeping through.

"Yeah, it looks about right. Here, take these strips and fold them up to put on top of the wounds along her shoulders. Then use some of the longer strips to wrap around on top of the makeshift bandages." Kat's Red Cross training was coming in handy.

As soon as Kat had turned eighteen, she had taken some advanced classes from the Red Cross. We needed to make sure someone in the family could take care of us, if we were ever injured during a hurricane and couldn't seek assistance.

"Joseph's on his way. We need to get moving. If there are as many vamps as I smell, Damien and Luke are going to need help. Kat, are you ready with some spells?" Rico put his phone back in his pocket and headed to the front door of the store.

I wasn't sure how I felt about leaving this girl here all alone. She was dying. Kat and I did what we could for her, but I still felt awful leaving her here to die alone. All I could do, at this point, was hope and pray Joseph made it here in time.

"I'm ready as I'll ever be." Kat clutched the messenger bag around her shoulders.

I reached into my bag to grab another stake since I lost one fighting with Alexy.

Rico nodded at me, and I nodded back. Even though I was still angry with him for how he treated me, I was very grateful he still had my back.

"How many storm girls are left?" Rico swayed his head from side to side, checking before we all walked out of the wooden gate in front of the glass door to the store.

"There should still be four more girls to save, if they haven't drained any of them dry yet." I shuddered recalling what it felt like to have so much blood viciously removed from my neck without my permission.

There were phantom pains running down my neck and shoulders as I tried very hard to get the image out of my mind. Less than a year ago, I was left in a warehouse to die as my attacker faced off against Rico, when he came to save me.

Joseph gave me a blood transfusion, which saved my life, after Rico and his pack tore the vamp to shreds. Seeing the poor girl lying on the ground made the experience fresh in my mind. It took a long time to get over the nightmares.

I hoped they wouldn't be returning.

Rico did a double-take when he looked at me. "Jenna, are you alright? You look terrified. Are you ready for this?"

"Yeah, I'm fine. Looking at the girl just brings back some scary memories. That's all." I tried to give him a smile, but it came out lopsided.

"I can take you outside in the sunlight, if you want to wait this out?" At least Rico wasn't insisting I sit it out this time.

"No, I can do it. Give me a second to get my head straight." After I took a deep breath, Rico gave me a hug.

"Thank you for asking instead of telling me to go outside." I whispered in Rico's ear.

He whispered back, "You're welcome. I'm trying, Jenna. Really, I am."

"I know, and I appreciate it."

"Alright you two, you can discuss this when we get those girls back and kill the vamps. Let's get a move on, there's not much daylight left. They're stuck here in the mall until the sun sets, then they will be gone, with the girls. Again." Kat was right. We needed to focus on the task at hand.

"Okay, I'm ready. Let's kick some demon butt!" This is what we have trained for. I knew I could do it.

"Follow me and stay close. Ignore the humans, unless you think they might be acolytes." Rico took point, and we followed him.

Kat and I scanned the area around us. Most of the stores had closed up. I could only see a few "Open" signs up.

"Rico, could they be inside any of the stores? Should we check each one?" I saw one store with a few people looking out into the mall. The sign said: "Closed." No one looked to be vampires. They all looked like frightened humans who couldn't look away from the scene of a gruesome accident.

"No, I want to find my guys before we do anything else. My guess is they are in the thick of things." Rico's head swiveled to the right. Just down the way was another wing of the mall off to the right side.

"I hear fighting down that way." Rico pointed to the right side-wing of the mall.

There was a large department store at the end. The walkway had multiple carts of small wares and trinkets. Then there were the shops which lined each side. There weren't any vacant stores down there the last time I was here.

Rico picked up his pace, and we tried to keep up. He was fast. Kat and I had to jog to keep up with his fast walk.

When we finished this, I needed to take up jogging.

After we turned down the lane, I saw what Rico heard. It was utter chaos.

Kat and I stopped to survey the situation.

"I see seven vamps and maybe three acolytes. What do you see, Kat?"

"I think there are four acolytes. Look at the one in the corner with the humans. He looks like he herded them there." She pointed to a group standing off to the left of the department store entrance. They were all stuck in a corner with one human standing guard.

"Is he keeping them there? Why? They're going to lose to the wolves. From the looks of it, they are already losing." I saw two vamp bodies on the ground. Both had their heads ripped off.

The storm girls were huddled in an alcove of a store. Three humans blocked them from leaving. The store behind them had their "Closed" sign up. One girl was knocking on the door and jiggling the door handle. It appeared to be locked.

"Rico, there are the girls. Kat and I will go over and incapacitate the acolytes guarding them." I grabbed Kat's hand and headed to the storm girls.

"Don't kill the men, if you can help it." Rico called over his shoulder before he jumped into the fray staying in his human form.

There were seven vampires fighting eight wolves. The men from Rico's pack had shifted and were fighting in their wolf form right in front of all of the humans still here. I couldn't tell who was who in wolf form. Rico had the only wolf form I knew for sure. He was the largest of his entire pack, so if I didn't already have his shifted body memorized, I could still pick him out.

I thought I might know which one was Damien. Theoretically, he should be the second largest wolf. There were two wolves who looked to be the same size. I wondered if they were Damien and Jose? All of the rest of the wolves were smaller than those two.

Rico was still in human form when he approached a vampire from behind. For a moment, I thought Rico might get the jump on him. At the last second, the blood-sucker whirled around so quickly it made me dizzy just watching.

I didn't recognize this vamp from the storage facility. He was a ginger and not quite as tall as Rico. He was wearing a t-shirt from the local university, promoting their baseball team. The mascot looked like Bluebeard the Pirate.

While I wanted to watch Rico kill the demon, I needed to focus on the storm girls and getting them away from the demented, vampire worshipers.

"Kat, can you get a pink spell between the girls and the

acolytes?" It would put up a force field to protect the girls while we took down the enemy.

"Sure, I can try. Will the spell activate as soon it hits the ground? Or does it wait until the stone has stopped moving?" Kat pulled out a pink spell stone.

"As soon as it hits the ground. Aim it for the corner of the store. Right were the alcove opens up to the entrance. It should give the girls enough space to stay safe until we take those three guys down." While I wasn't supposed to kill them, I certainly wouldn't cry if any died while we fought.

"Got it." She aimed for the corner and threw it, kinda like a large dice.

The pink stone hit right next to where I hoped it would and emitted a faint pink pulse before the shield went up. There was a very small space between the store's window and where the shield ended. It wasn't big enough for anyone to crawl through so I wasn't worried about it.

One of the acolytes tried barging through the field. He received a shock big enough to knock him out once he landed. The force of the shield threw him almost two feet away. He would be out for a while.

The guy on the floor had dark black hair. It was long, past his shoulders. He looked more like a flower child, or reject from Woodstock, than an acolyte.

"Guys, you can't stand up against us. The girls are safe from you. Stand down, and we won't harm you." Kat used her authoritative voice, hoping to keep from hurting anyone.

"We will fight until the death, if our masters wish it. Which they do. They are fighting to preserve our way of life, why shouldn't we fight?" A strong man with brown hair stood tall and proud as he spewed stupidity from his brain-washed mind.

"Try the violet stone. I want to see how it works on a

human." It did nothing for vamps. I should know since I tried it out back in the storage facility.

Kat pulled the violet stone from her hand was about to throw it when the force field went down. Without the protection of the field, the girls would be in danger.

"Screw this!" Kat yelled before turning on one of the bracelets. She ran at the two human acolytes left standing before they realized the shield was down.

Kat reached out and grabbed both of them by their shoulders. The charm she activated was one I had already used as well. It was a one-time use charm. Once she used it, that was it. No more magic would come from the bracelet.

Both vamp worshipers were electrocuted. They fell to the ground flopping uncontrollably and foam gathered in the corners of their mouths. With their eyes rolling to the back of their heads, I wondered if they were gagging on their tongues.

"Kat, Rico said not to kill them. We have to do something." I ran to the guy with brown hair and rolled him over on his stomach and foamy stuff came out of his mouth.

His body started to relax. After about a minute of flailing on the ground, both men stopped and gasped before passing out. At least I hope they passed out.

I reached down and felt for a pulse on his neck. It was weak, but there. I released a sigh, and I looked up into Kat's worried face. "He's alive."

"Bummer." Kat could be cold, but I understood where she was coming from.

"These guys are addicts. Which reminds me. Did you really want to feel a vampire bite you seductively?" I knew it wasn't the time or place to talk about it, but she had really shocked me earlier.

"I'll tell you all about it later. Just know I do NOT want to experience it, ever. I just knew he wouldn't be able to touch me with his fangs." Kat reached down and checked the pulse on the other acolyte. "He's alive too."

"What do we do? Stay here and protect the girls? Or join the fight?" I looked out and searched for Rico.

Kat turned around and watched the fighting. "I don't think they need us."

I watched as Rico beheaded a vampire with his bare hands. Although, to be fair, a part of its neck was ripped out. One of the wolves must have started it, and Rico finished it.

Two wolves sprawled on the ground panting. Red blood stained their coats.

Three of the vampires were down for the count, and add in the decapitated one Rico just dropped, there were only three blood-suckers left to deal with. It should be easy.

One of the largest wolves, Damien I think, was fighting the ginger. The vamp's clawed hand grazed the wolf's snout. Damien rammed into the vamp's stomach and pushed him close to us.

The ginger turned around and smiled at me. He lunged for me before Kat could throw up a shield.

He had his hand wrapped around my throat. "Oh, Rico. You might want to see what I captured."

"Let her go, now! Or I will stake you to the ground right before the sun rises and watch as you slowly burn to ash with the rising dawn." Rico stalked closer to us and left the vampire behind him.

The vamp tried to grab onto Rico, but lost his focus, and one of the wolves jumped him and ripped out his neck.

"Your mangy mutt really shouldn't have done that. I think Jenna's going to pay for your impertinence. Tell your pack to stand down. Give me back my acolytes, all of them.

Or I will kill Jenna right here in front of you." The vampire holding me sniffed my neck.

Gross! Why do they always do that? Can they smell my blood?

"You can't bite her. She's protected by a very strong spell. It would repel any vampire who would bite her." Rico inched closer to us. I couldn't see Kat, I hoped she was figuring out a way to kill this guy before he could hurt me.

"I'll wait for her magic to wear off. She doesn't have the strength to power it for long." I saw out of the corner of my eye a smug expression on his face. Too bad he was mistaken.

"It won't wear off. A very strong witch protected all four of the dolls. He used his own essence in the spell creation." Now Rico had the smug look on his face.

Ginger's grasp tightened on my neck and cut off my air supply. I scrapped at his hands, but he didn't let go, until I almost passed out. "Interesting. I can't bite you my dear, but I can strangle you." His grip loosened a little bit, enough to let some much needed air into my lungs.

"Rico, do as I say, or she dies right here. Pity, it would be a waste of such sweet blood." The ginger cackled. He actually sounded like one of those crazy cartoon witches.

"Don't, Rico!" I gasped out.

I winked at him hoping he would get the hint. I had a plan.

The ginger used his left hand to hold my neck. I used my right hand and started hitting him. I knew he would use his free hand to grab mine. When he did, I reached my other hand into my pocket and pulled out a spell stone.

It was a yellow one.

I wasn't sure if the vamp noticed, but I know Rico did. When I tried hitting the vamp again, Rico moved forward. He was less than two feet away now.

This was going to hurt. A lot.

After taking a deep breath, I slammed the stone from my hand into the ginger's thigh.

I held my breath and closed my eyes as I felt the concussive blast tear me out of the vampire's grasp and throw me into the waiting arms of Rico.

Ginger was blown back against the windows of the store. Kat was ready and staked him in his heart the moment he landed. The guy probably didn't even see it coming. Those concussive blasts tended to knock vampires out.

My entire body was on fire. Not a single place on my body held no pain. If Rico hadn't of caught me, I probably would have cracked my head open on the ground when I landed. As it was, I felt blood dripping from my nose, and my ears were ringing.

Rico held me in his arms as the world around me went black.

29

JENNA

*L*ight was trying to make its way into my eyes. I felt my eyelashes fluttering, probably the only part of my body which didn't hurt. The rest of it was a dull pain.

"She's waking up. Call Rico in here." I heard a male voice. It sounded soothing and familiar.

"Jenna, can you hear me?" There it was again. The sound of an angel. I felt a soothing sensation envelope my entire body, and the dull ache went away.

I tried to talk, but my mouth was so dry, it felt like the Sahara Desert.

"Shh. It's alright. You're safe now." Another voice said as he took my hand in his. It felt so warm, so right. I sighed my contentment.

I felt a hand brush away my bangs, and a moment later, someone kissed my forehead. "Oh, Jenna. You scared me something awful. Why did you use the concussive spell? You almost died."

I didn't know what he was talking about. I squeezed his hand before I fell back into nothingness.

"*J*enna, can you hear me?" The voice from earlier was back.

I knew him. My eyelashes fluttered and this time I was able to open my eyes. Next to me sat a gorgeous man. One I knew protected me.

What did he protect me from?

"R...Rico?" My throat felt like sandpaper, scratching the wrong way.

"Shh, don't talk. You're safe. Here, drink some water." He lifted me forward just a bit and held a cup of water with a straw in front of me.

I took the straw between my lips and sucked. It felt like new life was flowing through my body. I continued to drink, and my throat started to feel better.

"That's enough. You have to take it slow." Rico pulled the cup away from me.

"What happened?" I said hoarsely.

"You used a concussive spell on a vampire who was holding you. Thank heavens I was close enough to catch you when the blast expelled you away from his body." I felt Rico holding my hand, and a small smile automatically pulled at the corners of my mouth.

"Please don't do that again. Kat was making her way to stake the vamp. If you would have waited thirty seconds, she probably would have gotten him." He pulled my hand up to his face and kissed the back of it. A ripple of pleasure shot out from my heart.

"Thank you for catching me." I cleared my throat, and it felt better. I also sounded better. "I didn't know Kat was coming up behind me. It's coming back. He was going to strangle me."

I reached my free hand up to my throat, and it was tender to the touch. I winced and pulled my hand away.

"He did try to strangle you. When you used the spell, it wrenched his hand away from your throat and caused more damage. You're lucky the witch's council likes your moxy. Joseph called and asked for a healer." Rico's eyes blurred up. He looked like he was about to cry.

"How long have I been out?" If a witch healed me, I probably was still in the mall.

I looked around at my surroundings for the first time. This wasn't the mall. I was in a bedroom, not mine. It was Joseph's. I was in the twin bed he used the last time a vamp almost killed me.

"You've been out for almost a week. If you hadn't used so much magic, it probably would have taken a day for your body to heal. The witch who came by, Alaric, cautioned us all on the overuse of Magic." Rico leaned over and kissed my forehead again.

He put his forehead against mine. "Jenna, please promise me you won't overdo the magic again. I won't be able to handle losing you."

I brought my free hand up to cup his face. "Rico, I learned my lesson. I will only use what I have to in order to save my life, or the lives of others. No more. And I promise to take a few days in between."

"Thank you. Your sisters are worried sick about you. They're waiting in the other room to see you."

"Wait, how was Kat? She used several spells in the mall. Is she alright?" I couldn't remember how many she used, but it had to be close to what I used.

"She didn't suffer any ill side-effects. She slept for twelve hours when we returned, and then when she woke up, she was totally fine. Alaric thinks it might have to do with her shifter blood. She can probably handle more magic use than you, Sam, or Indie. So just keep this in mind, if you think you can keep up with her. You can't. She has magic in her DNA. All paranormal creatures do." Rico stood up and kissed my hand before laying it down on my stomach.

"I'll get your sisters. They're going to be so excited to see you awake." Rico turned and opened the door.

When the door opened, I heard screaming and crying in the other room.

"Oh, thank Buddha!" Indie yelled.

"No, thank God! He's the one who healed her." Sam countered.

All three of my sisters practically ran into my room.

"Jenna! You're awake! We wondered if you would ever wake up." Kat sat on the chair Rico had been using. Sam and Indie stood next to her.

"Hi, there. Can someone tell me what happened after I blacked out? Did we save the girls? Kill the vamps?" I had been out for almost a week and had no clue what happened with the fight.

I was pretty sure I remembered Kat staking the ginger vampire after I used the yellow spell stone and nothing after that. My mind was a complete blank.

"Of course. Did you see me stake the vamp with the red hair?" Kat's eyes sparkled with her excitement.

"Yes, that's the last thing I remember."

"The red-head must have been their leader because once the remaining vamps saw what I did to him, they lost their fight. Rico and his pack easily killed them, after questioning them."

"What did he find out? Were they rogues? Or was the queen involved?" I remembered something from when I was at Castle Storage. It sounded like they might be rogues.

Although, I doubted the queen was oblivious to what they were doing.

"Turns out the queen didn't even know this group. Well, one had been kicked out of the local coven a few years ago. He went on a blood binge around the country and picked up his own coven. These were all untrained vamps who thought they could do whatever they wanted."

"No way!" I couldn't believe it. This was a pretty large group to go unnoticed.

"They moved around from state to state, even spent some time in Canada and Mexico before coming back here. Their favorite snack food was freshman girls. They left a trail of drained bodies all over North America, until we killed them all."

"Did Rico tell the vampire queen about this?" I wondered how she took it?

"He did. She was grateful we killed them all for her. If we hadn't, and she learned about them, she was honor-bound to hunt and kill them all. No one is allowed to create a coven and not train them properly. It's grounds for staking." Kat seemed very excited over this news.

"I'm guessing there's more? You seem very giddy." I tried to sit up further in my bed but needed help.

Kat assisted me in getting situated before continuing. "The local witch's coven was so impressed with what we did they want to give us some more spells. We will get to keep using magic as long as we continue to train and promise to not overuse the spells."

"Wow! That's huge!" I was shocked. Why would they want to keep supplying us with magic?

"They are even going to make us more charm bracelets with the force field in them. The leader of the coven promised to make them last longer, too. They still won't be rechargeable, but we can protect ourselves better. If you'd had another one of those bracelets, the redhead never would have gotten ahold of you." Kat did have some seriously great news to share.

I was flabbergasted. "Okay, so tell me about the rest of the fight? And what happened to the girls?"

"There really wasn't a fight after you passed out. The wolves quickly killed three more vamps. The rest asked for lenience. As if." Kat snorted, and Sam and Indie laughed.

They really didn't have any training. All vamps should know the penalty for what they did was death. No matter who you were.

"And the girls? Are they going to be alright?" I couldn't imagine what they were going through. They would probably never finish school, at least not here.

Indie began telling me about the girls, "They're going to be fine. All of them were seriously low on blood, not surprisingly. So they all received transfusions when the ambulances arrived."

"One has already been released. She went home. I think she's going to transfer to a school closer to home next year and take the rest of this year off. In fact, all of the girls have requested to be pulled from classes. I can't blame them." Indie was wringing her hands in front of her body. She did this when she was really upset or nervous. It was one of her tells.

"The rest of the girls are still in the hospital?" It would be surprising if they were.

"Yes, they seem to be having a difficult time processing. Joseph has sent a psychologist to visit them. He knows about vampires and everything. They are getting the best possible treatment, but it's going to be a slow road." Sam sighed and looked down at her hands.

"I wish there was something we could do for them." Other than talking to them, I doubted we could help in any way, no matter how much I wanted to.

"What about all of the witnesses? Aren't they claiming to have seen wolves fighting vamps?

"Actually, there was a gas leak. It seems the hurricane left some damage at the mall after all." Kat smirked.

"Nice cover story. I guess is helps to explain the crazy visions they all saw." It's too bad we couldn't tell the world the truth.

The public couldn't handle it. Choosing to believe a gas leak caused someone to hallucinate vampires and were-wolves, doesn't seem right. I bet, somewhere deep down inside, they know the truth. They are just choosing to bury it.

What a crazy week it's been! A cat 2 hurricane skirted around NOLA, I was almost kidnapped twice by deranged vampires, and only five of the eight missing girls survived the storm.

"What's next?" Sometimes I felt like I was living in a cartoon.

"We train. Keep learning all we can about this new world and kill all vamps who don't follow the rules. The last part is my favorite." I think we created a monster in Kat.

EPILOGUE

JENNA

"I can't believe it's been two weeks since you almost died, Jenna." Rico just couldn't let it alone.

He kept reminding me of this fact every day since I woke up.

"Rico, come on. Stop it. I don't need to be reminded on a daily basis of the fact I almost died. I can't think of much else."

"I'm sorry. It's just, well...I keep seeing you lying in the bed with your eyes closed and unresponsive to everything. I went nuts the week you were out of it. Can you blame me?" He tilted his head and looked into my eyes with such intensity. It caused my heart to pitter patter like a stormy night.

We were in my garage. It was the only place we could talk without being interrupted. Since I woke up, we had not been left alone for more than a couple of minutes.

Not because anyone was afraid we would do anything fun, it was because my sisters couldn't stand to be away from me for more than a few minutes. They were constantly hovering and asking me if I needed anything. It was exhausting.

"Rico, I know I screwed up a few times since meeting you. The last encounter with vampires has taught me I have soooo much to learn still." I paced the small area of my garage where we stored our band equipment.

We hadn't had a gig in a few weeks and it was really starting to bother me. Kat refused to book anything until Rico gave her the green light regarding my health.

"I won't use much magic going forward. In fact, I have learned magic doesn't always help. Sometimes, it can be harmful. When can I start my kung-fu training again? Rico hated it when I called martial arts training "kung-fu." I loved messing with him.

"Jenna...you know Martial Arts training is not called kung-fu. Why can't you learn the proper terms?" With a frustrated sigh, he ran a hand through his hair, showing off his muscled forearms.

While trying to keep from laughing, I reached up and put my arms behind his head. The feel of his hair between my fingers sent chills down my spine. "Rico, you know I love to mess with you. My sisters have already started back up with their routines. I'm ready. I don't want to wait any longer or I'll get too far behind."

"I'll help you catch up if you do." Rico wrapped his arms around my waist.

I looked up from beneath my fluttering eyelashes and said in a whisper, "Plus, I miss rolling around on the mats with you."

Rico moaned and put his forehead against mine. "I just want to make sure your back to one hundred percent before taxing your body so much. I couldn't handle it if something happened to you, again."

"Then we'll take it slowly." A smile slowly developed as I

thought about other things I wanted to take slowly with him.

Rico closed his eyes and inched his lips closer to mine. I could feel his hot breath against my lips right before he lightly brushed a kiss on them.

I returned the soft kiss which turned into a smoldering, hot kiss very quickly. Tingles covered my body from head to toe. This kiss felt like it had the power to curl my toes.

"Knock-knock." Aleric called out when he walked into my garage, interrupting my first kiss with Rico mid-toe curl.

"Oh! Sorry, man. I had no idea." Aleric said as he backed away and looked anywhere but at us.

"What did you need?" Rico barked.

I could feel his body tense up. Mine did too. It was the first time we had been alone for more than five minutes. He had finally kissed me! Some stupid witch had to go and interrupt us before Rico could even begin to deepen the kiss.

"Truly, I'm sorry. I hadn't realized you two finally got over yourselves. I guess a near death experience can do that, huh?" Aleric was babbling and still couldn't look at us.

My face was burning up. It was such an embarrassing situation to be caught in. I hoped my face wasn't red.

"The witch's council has requested your presence tomorrow." Aleric was standing in the doorway to my garage.

"You could have just sent me a text. Why the in person invite?" Rico dropped his arms from around my waist and stepped away from me.

"I'm sorry I wasn't clear. The invite is for Jenna and the Dolls." Aleric looked up to me.

My eyes opened wide. "Oh? Why us?"

"The council no longer has faith in the vampire queen. They have a proposition for you and your sisters. Please join us tomorrow in council chambers at five o'clock." Aleric looked over to Rico. "You are invited, if you wish to attend."

"Thank you, Aleric. I will attend. Does this mean the entire council will be present?" Rico narrowed his eyes before taking hold of my hand and squeezing it.

"No. It isn't an official meeting. The head of the council thought it would be easier if you met in chambers. It is a confidential meeting. Please tell no one else, and I think you should bring your sisters with you, even though Jenna was technically the one invited." Aleric turned around and left before I could even respond to his request.

"Rico, do you know what's going on?" I scratched my head and blinked a few times.

"War is coming."

The End

I hope you enjoyed Hurricane of Magic! Book 3, Council of Magic is now available!

Keep reading for a special excerpt from the newest book in this series!

*J*oin my Newsletter where you will get a free book as well as a notice when my latest books go up for sale or pre-sale.
https://jlhendricksauthor.com/newsletter/

*T*here are two novella prequels currently available!
If you join my newsletter, you will receive *The Voodoo That You Do*. This short story tells the tale of what happens to men when they cheat on Indie! She's the best

voodoo doll maker there is! Any guy would be foolish to mess with her!

Magic's Not Real. It's the prequel which tells the story of the vampire who tried to kill Jenna with a death curse! It also shows how the Dolls met Rico and his pack. While technically this story takes place after The Voodoo That You Do, you could read either of these stories in any order.

*I*nterested in staying up to date on the latest with The Voodoo Dolls? Or want to see what else I write? Check out my social media accounts where you can find more about my writing as well as special offers and promotions I love to share!

Facebook: https://www.facebook.com/JLHendricksAuthor/

Twitter: https://twitter.com/TinkFan25

On Twitter you just might catch Indie and Jenna going back and forth with Voodoo Dolls! Sam even joins in once in a while. But watch out for Indie (aka Aysia Amery)! She can be ruthless!

Blog: http://jlhendricksauthor.com/blog/

Follow me on BookBub if you just want new release notices: https://www.bookbub.com/authors/j-l-hendricks

SNEAK PEEK OF THE VOODOO THAT YOU DO

Men, be very careful when dating a woman who makes voodoo dolls for a living. You just might live to regret your mistakes.

Indie and her three adopted sisters, the Voodoo Dolls, run a tourist shop in New Orleans, Louisiana (NOLA). They are also The Voodoo Dolls, an indie rock band who don't believe magic is real.

Voodoo dolls are just tchotchkes, right? A fun pin cushion which allows you to pretend you're really hurting the object of your ire.

But what happens when Indie's boyfriend cheats on her, and she creates a voodoo doll that represents him? Using his own hair and a toenail clipping, Indie sets about to seek revenge for the pain Brian caused her. Only to discover that Voodoo Magic just might be real!

Indie

"Alright! That last set rocked the house! Kat, spring break is around the corner, what gigs do you have lined up for us?" I asked our band manager and lead guitarist.

"We have three gigs each week this April. Until then, we have to focus on practice, girls. Indie, you might need to let Brian know you're going to be really busy for the next few weeks. Remember, this is our future." Kat put her guitar into her case as we all packed up our equipment from tonight's gig.

It was a minor club, but it was packed! Most of the front of the stage was filled with our fans who follow us from club to club. Sam, one of my sisters, is our web diva. She makes sure that everyone knows where we are performing and when. I can usually recognize a decent amount of fans at each club we play.

I know that if we can double our fan base, we should be able to get a record contract. Twelve gigs in April should really get us out there and help to attract more fans, which in turn, will attract the record executives. The four of us have worked extremely hard to get where we are now.

Kat started our band five years ago and has worked her butt off to get us within striking distance of our goal. The extra income hasn't hurt either.

"Can Brian come watch us practice? He started out as a fan, you know." Brian and I had only been dating a few months, but it seemed to be getting serious. He had talked about us taking the next step just last week. I hope that meant he was considering proposing to me. *Was I ready for marriage?*

"Sure, as long as he doesn't distract you." Kat walked over to help me take down my drum set.

"I just hope you two can keep your hands off each other. Last time he came over I about puked when I walked in on you two in the kitchen. He practically had your entire face in his mouth! Talk about gross!" Jenna started to laugh as she coiled up the cord for her mic.

"What about when I walked in on them in the garage? I swear! They can't keep their lips apart! It's like you two super-glued your mouths together. Disgusting!" Sam shook her head and picked up her guitar case.

Jenna was the lead singer, and Sam played bass guitar. Both were the best singers I had ever heard.

"Oh, please! You're all just jealous you don't have hot boyfriends. Just admit it." I threw a drumstick at Jenna who screeched and dodged the stick.

"Who has time for a boyfriend right now? Between running our shop and our band, there isn't any time for a guy. At least, not a serious one. How many times have I covered your shifts at The Voodoo Dolls Store, just so you could spend time with your guy? He isn't even that cute." Sam wrinkled her nose. She had never really liked Brian.

From the moment I introduced him to the group, she was always a bit standoffish. I thought she may have had a crush on him. We had all noticed him in the crowds of the bars we performed. He seemed to follow us around.

Brian was a rarity. He had brown hair with hints of natural auburn highlights. His hair had that just got out of bed look, and he rocked it! Those smoky-blue eyes of his could see into my soul. I would spend hours just gazing into his perfectly chiseled face and wonder how I got so lucky.

Sam said he had a different girl each time she saw him. That didn't bother me. It just meant none of them were serious girls. He must have been waiting for me.

I looked out into the crowd and saw Brian. He was waiting by the bar, talking to a tall redhead.

"If you aren't careful, someone else will be taking the next step with him instead of you." Sam pointed to Brian and the home-wrecker.

I scrunched my nose and said, "Her? You've got to be kidding. She's probably just some chick he knows from work or something." I watched as he laughed, and she put her hand on his arm.

He saw me and took a step back from her, then said something and made his way to me.

"Hey, babe. Great set as usual! When are you girls going to start singing some new material? Isn't that the same line-up from your last four gigs?" Brian smiled up to me from the edge of the stage.

I jumped down to give him a kiss. "I know. We have several new songs we're going to introduce in our line-up for spring break. Kat is going to have us practicing a lot over the next couple of weeks. I'm not sure how much time I'll have for dates, but you can come and hang out with us during practices, like you used to."

"We'll see. Work is picking up too. I might have a few late nights and some weekend work prepping for a new ad campaign." He shrugged.

"Oh, hmm. Can you help us carry the equipment out to our van?" I pointed my thumb over my shoulder, indicating all of the heavy equipment we had packed up and ready to go.

"Sure, just let me say goodnight to some friends, and I'll come help you." Brian kissed my forehead and turned back toward the redhead and her friends.

"Huh, so he's going back to the redhead? Why isn't he helping us? He always does," Kat asked.

"He's going to say goodnight to his friends, then he'll come help. Come on. Let's get started." I bit my lip and reached up to have Kat and Jenna help me get back on stage.

It took twenty minutes for Brian to say goodnight to his friends. We had already loaded the van when he showed up.

"I'm so sorry, babe. Those were work friends. I talked them into coming and watching the show. They weren't ready to leave and kept talking to me. I totally lost track of time."

"I see. Well, you can come back with us and help unload, right?" I wrapped my arms around his neck and nibbled on his ear.

Breathing heavily, he answered, "Most definitely." Then he kissed me like he hadn't seen me in weeks, instead of hours.

"Oh, gross! Come on, Indie. We're all tired and want to get back to unload so we can go to sleep." Jenna covered her eyes and stuck her tongue out.

"Just wait, Jenna. When you get a boyfriend, I'm going to have a lot of fun paying you back." I smirked and grabbed Brian's hand.

End of Sneak Peek

Join my newsletter and you will receive a free copy of The Voodoo That You Do.

SNEAK PEEK- MAGIC'S NOT REAL

When magic IS real, what would you do to protect yourself?

Jenna and her three adopted sisters, the Voodoo Dolls, run a tourist shop in New Orleans, Louisiana (NOLA). They are also The Voodoo Dolls, an indie rock band who don't believe magic is real.

That is until someone tries to kill Jenna using a death curse. Rico and his pack are there when it happens. They decide to protect Jenna and the Dolls, while going after the evil that tried to kill the beautiful lead singer.

What the dolls don't realize is that everything from their nightmares is true! When they discover magic IS real, they all discover the terrible truth about vampires, shifters, and magic wielders. Will Jenna survive the evil which is after her? Will she be able to accept the assistance of a wolf shifter and his pack? Or will she fall prey to the creatures that live in the night.

Jenna

"Welcome to the Voodoo Doll's House. How can I help you?" I asked the latest patron who entered my shop.

"I was looking for a charm." The young, pretty blonde woman looked around and slowly walked to the counter. "I, um, well. You see, my boyfriend is cheating on me, and I want to either make him pay or get him to stop cheating. I don't know which yet. Can you help me?" The young, twenty-ish girl with wide, blue eyes, looked at me, and asked, "What can I do? I heard you make the best voodoo dolls in all of NOLA. Should I punish him?"

"Hm, yes, I see." I tapped my chin and thought for a moment. "Do you love him?"

"Yes, with everything I am."

"Then you don't want revenge or punishment, you want him to love you in return. I have just the thing." I walked to the other side of the small store and picked up a sachet of leaves and flowers, then handed it to my new eager client.

"This is a tea that you brew and serve to the one you love. If your love for him is true, he'll love you forever." I winked at her. "However, if your love isn't true, well, let's just say that you might want to think twice before you give him this tea." I frowned and watched her face for a reaction.

"Why? Will he hurt me or something?" Her eyes went wide.

"Not physically, but emotionally it will be quite painful. I must warn you. Only a few of my clients have actually come back to tell me that their journey ended in wedded bliss. Think long and hard about how you really feel for him. If you decide you love him - really and truly love him, like there would be no tomorrow without him, brew him this tea. You must drink it together and finish it while it's still hot."

My business partner and best friend, Indie, came through the back door and watched as the young woman ate up every word I said. "Oh, really? He'll propose and everything? Never cheat on me again?"

"If your love is true, yes." I nodded my head.

"Oh yes! I know exactly how I feel. I want him forever and ever! Tonight, I'll make him a special dinner, and then we can have tea with dessert! Tony - that's my boyfriend's name - isn't really a tea kinda guy, but I'll get him to drink it." The customer reached into the basket and grabbed five more bags of the tea before turning to follow me to the register.

"Miss, you won't need more than one bag of tea. If it doesn't work the first time, it won't work." I smiled at her, and when the lady turned to put the tea bags away, I winked at Indie.

Whirling back around, the young lady questioned, "Oh, can I buy these for my friends? Do they make nice gifts? I have several girlfriends who are having trouble with their boyfriends or husbands. Yvette's husband has already cheated once, that we know of, and she could really use this, too." The customer furrowed her brow and held on tight to the tea sachets.

"Of course, they make fantastic gifts! I have some gift bags you could use too. How about an aphrodisiac to go with them? We have a fresh batch of fudge, my partner Indie, made just this morning. If your man isn't in the mood, this will certainly help him get there, if you know what I mean." I raised my eyebrows and walked to the next counter to grab six sets of wrapped fudge, one set for the customer and the rest for her friends.

"Is there anything else you need help with?" I put the packages of dark chocolate and nuts, wrapped in red paper with a white bow, on the counter in front of my new client.

The woman looked around, hunched her shoulders and whispered, "Can I try the fudge first? I mean, does it taste weird once you put your voodoo in it?"

I put a hand over her mouth and giggled. "Of course you can taste it, but it must be a very small portion as it doesn't take much to get the magic working." I cut off a sliver of one of the bars of fudge and handed it to the woman.

"Mmm, that is really good. Does the magic or voodoo or whatever you do make it taste better? Cuz that is some of the best fudge I've ever had." She licked her lips and her eyes rolled back as she sighed.

"Huh, I hadn't thought of it before. But then again, I don't eat the fudge." I winked at the customer.

I rang up the purchase and said, "That will be $109.59, please."

The lady pulled out her credit card and giggled. "Oh, right! That would be awful to eat the fudge and have to stay here at work the rest of the day, wouldn't it?" The woman smiled when she handed her credit card over and gladly paid the bill.

"I guess a hundred dollars is cheap compared to the counseling bills some couples have, or the divorce attorneys!" The lady shivered.

The bell on the door rang as the smiling customer walked out the door. She had no clue she just paid over one hundred dollars for a simple rose tea and ordinary chocolate fudge. Those same items could be purchased for less than ten dollars at the grocery store.

"How do you always get them to spend over one hundred dollars? That lady came in looking for one thing, and you sent her out of here with twelve different items, including fancy gift bags." Indie shook her head.

"It's a gift." I shrugged and went back to sorting the new voodoo dolls we all made the night before.

That night I headed to Bourbon Street with my three best friends and roommates. We were the Voodoo Doll Sisters, a hot and popular indie rock band. At least one night a week we played in various clubs around the French Quarter in New Orleans, or NOLA as the locals called it. Our gig that night was at Bourbon on the Rocks, one of the most popular clubs in the French Quarter of New Orleans.

Kat, the oldest of our quartet at only twenty-five, smacked her gum while she drove the van to the club. "Ladies, I know we're headed to a major recording deal if we can just get in front of the right people!" She spent most of her spare time researching the agents and where they liked to hang out on Bourbon Street.

"I found a booking for a group of recording executives from a large New York agency. They'll be here in just a couple of months for a conference. If we can get our band booked to play even one gig in front of them, they'll be begging us to sign on the dotted line." She slapped the steering wheel.

Indie asked, "How'd you find out?" She blew a bubble while twirling the long pink strands of hair mixed in with her natural blonde locks that went down to the middle of her back.

"Hmph, while you girls were flirting with the bouncers at the last few clubs we played, I was schmoozing all of the booking agents. In the process, I was able to get our band booked into a few of the hottest clubs in town, Bourbon on the Rocks, being one of them." She eyed Indie over her shoulder before looking back at the road.

I was in the front passenger seat and laughed. "You mean you made out with all the booking agents in town!" I put my hand up for Indie, who gave me a high five.

Kat sat up straight. "Not all women have to use sex to get what they want. I happen to be extremely good at needling men until they give me what I want." She pursed her lips and kept her eyes on the road. Kat was beautiful. She was 5' 7" with long brunette hair. We all died strands of our hair different colors, hers was electric blue. Which helped her blue eyes to stand out even more.

"Oh come on, Kat. Don't be mad. Jenna was just teasing you. We all know you're the best at negotiations, which is why you're the band's manager." Sam replied. She was the fourth member of the band. At twenty-one, she was also the youngest.

"Exactly! Kit Kat, I know you would never do anything like that just to get us gigs. We're all too talented to sell ourselves for bookings." I twisted in my seat so I could reach over and pat Kat's shoulder.

Kat shook herself and said, "Alright Dolls, this is it! If we kill it tonight, we've got it! I think we should do that new song."

"Not tonight, Kat. It isn't ready. I don't want to play that one until we have it perfected." Sam exclaimed.

"Sam, you know that song better than any of us! Are you saying that we aren't ready for it?" I turned around, tilted my head, and looked at my younger band mate.

Sam's eyes opened wide and she shook her hands in front of her. "Uh, ah... NO! I would never say that. You guys are all so much better than I am. It's just that, I don't feel comfortable with the song yet. You know I need more time for new music, to feel it and learn it intimately. I can't just pick up an instrument and play something like Indie does." She pursed her lips and looked at her hands in her lap.

"Oh no you don't! You're practically a one-woman-show Sam. You can play any instrument you touch. None of us can do that. And if you weren't so shy, you'd probably be the lead singer. Right girls?" Indie put her arm around her best friend and adopted sister.

"I would be more than happy to play guitar and be back-up vocals, Sam. You just say the word, and you can front the band." I was the lead singer of the band and on occasion played the guitar.

"And have all those guys staring at me? No way! I'll stick with my bass and being ignored. All of the guys want the lead singer or the chicks who play drums." Sam shook her head. We all knew she was wrong, but we decided to let her live in her bubble.

"I say we do it. Sam you've already perfected the song. What more do you need? Come on, it's totally awesome and those record guys will love it!" I poked Sam in the arm and smiled at her before turning back around to look out the front window.

Sam couldn't resist smiling back. "Alright, Jenna. But I warn you. I don't feel like I really have it yet."

Kat activated the left turn signal to pull down the back alley of the club. "Sam, you have this. You're the only one who can play the song on all instruments. I've heard you sing the entire thing by yourself, and I was moved to dance. Girl, you got chops. Don't ever let yourself think you don't."

We all hopped out of our dusty blue 1969 Ford conversion van as soon as Kat stopped it behind the club. "Man, this old rust bucket sure has seen us through a lot." Indie ran her hand along the dented rear fender. "I remember this dent. Kat, you were teaching me to drive back when I was only fifteen." Indie smiled and patted the van.

"What's with the reminiscing, Indie? That was ages ago. Come on, we have to unload this bucket of bolts and get set up before we go on in," Kat looked at her wristwatch. "Thirty minutes! Let's get a move on girls. Fame and fortune wait for no one."

"Except the Voodoo Dolls!" We all chimed in together. It was our mantra. One day, we would have both fame and fortune.

I peeked through the red velour curtain that hid us while we set up our equipment on stage. My eyebrows rose and my mouth formed an "O".

"What? Who's out there?" Kat asked.

"The place is packed, wall to wall muscle! It's full of men with arms the size of my thighs!" I pointed to my purple fishnet stockings that matched the color of my hair. "Looks like a convention of body builders. It's standing room only out there." I pointed to what lay beyond the curtain separating us from the testosterone filled room.

"Kat, where are all of the women? The only females I see are the waitresses," I asked when I opened the curtain just enough to peek one eyeball through the only thing protecting us from all of those men.

Kat walked over to the curtain and peered out. "Don't worry. It's a party of some sort tonight. A closed party in fact. The owner assured me there would be recording guys here tonight too. Just relax and enjoy all of the hot guys checking you out." Kat nudged me to take my place.

It was odd playing in one of my favorite clubs. This was our second time performing here and it was just as nerve-racking as the first time.

After taking her place stage left, Kat tuned her electric guitar. I stopped before taking my position center stage. Indie, the group's free spirit, walked up to the front of the stage. She opened the curtain and stepped out.

"Hiya!" Indie winked at a table of men who were ogling her. She blew them a kiss then turned around and strutted to her drums.

The men whistled and pounded the tables as they downed their shot glasses of amber liquid.

"That's how it's done, sister. Now get your butt out there and get things started." Indie smacked my backside, then I yelped and jumped.

I took my spot in the front and nodded to the stage hand who started to open the curtains. Then Indie counted "One, two, three, slamming her sticks together before launching into our first song of the night.

End of Sneak Peek

Magic's Not Real is available on Amazon

ALSO BY J.L. HENDRICKS

Interested in what took place before this book started? Check out the prequels currently available and keep reading for a sneak peek of each!

The Voodoo That You Do is available inside Midnight Magic for a limited time!

This is the story of Indie and what happens when her boyfriend cheats on her! Men, be very careful when you date a woman who claims to have mad voodoo power!

Magic's Not Real is available on Amazon!

This is Jenna's story. Find out what happened when a magic flinging vampire tried to kill her with a death curse!

Other Books by J.L. Hendricks

The Voodoo Dolls

Book 0: The Voodoo That You Do

Book 0.5: Magic's Not Real

Book 1: New Orleans Magic

Book 2: Hurricane of Magic

Book 3: Council of Magic

Alpha Alien Abduction Tales Series

Book 0: Worlds Revealed (join my Newsletter to get this exclusive freebie)

Book 1: Worlds Away

Book 2: Worlds Collide

Book 2.5: Worlds Explode

Book 3: Worlds Entwined

A Shifter Christmas Romance Series

Book 0: Santa Meets Mrs. Claus

Book 1: Miss Claus and the Secret Santa

Book 2: Miss Claus under the Mistletoe

Book 3: Miss Claus and the Christmas Wedding (Christmas 2018)

The FBI Dragon Chronicles

Book 1: A Ritual of Fire

Book 2: A Ritual of Death

The Original Eclipse Series

Book 0: Eclipse of the Beginning

Book 1: Eclipse of the Warrior

Book 2: Eclipse of Power (coming soon)

Book 3: Eclipse of the Heart (coming soon)

See these titles and more at https://www.jlhendricksauthor.com/

NEWSLETTER SIGN-UP

If you want to make sure you hear about the latest and greatest, sign up for my newsletter at: https://jlhendricksauthor.com/newsletter/ I will only send out a few e-mails a month. Also, you will get a free book just for signing up!

ACKNOWLEDGMENTS

Writing a book takes more than just the author. This is a team effort all the way around! I originally had two covers for this one book. The designer I contracted with to do the series was so busy, I had to wait until the book was done to get the cover. So I contacted my regular designer, Victoria Cooper, and asked her for help with getting a temp cover so I could put up the book for pre-sale. She did such a great job, I decided to make it the cover for a prequel book. So, if you bought an early copy of this book, don't worry about losing the fantastic cover Victoria did because it will be on the Magic's Not Real.

Rebecca Frank has been contracted to do all three covers! She is fantastic and highly sought after. The only downside is she had a very long waitlist. But it's worth it to wait for her covers as they are a work of art! Thanks Becky for such a great series of covers!!

Editing is the one part I hate. LOL I have a wonderful and talented developmental editor. Rebecca Reddell has been with me for a while now, which is really nice. She has gotten to know my style so well, and has taught me a ton about writing. Rebecca used to be an English Teacher! Yikes! She is also an indie author. I think her insight into how to write is something which has taught me more than getting a degree in creative writing would do for me. Thank you Becky for working hard and always delivering, even when I don't give you much time!

Beta readers are the last line. After Becky does my edits, I run over the story and always add more, or take away. Since I don't send it back to my editor, I use Beta readers. They read the story and catch typos, grammatical errors, and sometimes even some inconsistency issues. I'm not perfect. I can mess things up after the re-writes I do. A huge thank you goes out to Leo Roars, Sandy Kirnbauer, and Kathy Miller! Thank you so much for getting this turned around so quickly!

AUTHOR'S NOTES

Thank you so much for reading the second book in my latest series, The Voodoo Dolls! I hope you are enjoying it half as much as I'm enjoying the writing of this series! Book 3 is already out, so go ahead and grab your copy on Amazon!

Jenna and the Dolls are still learning. They have more growing to do. We all do, really. I don't think anyone in real life ever stops learning, at least, I hope they don't. What I am enjoying about this series is how much Jenna and her sisters grow. They were just normal young adults until a huge event. Then, they learned magic was real, and so were all of the scary stories they learned growing up.

Now, my Voodoo Dolls are starting to fight back, and win! They have some setbacks, and a lot to still learn, but they are moving forward.

Keep an eye out on Kat in the next book. I haven't given you much about her yet and her story. It's still developing in my brain. I had an epiphany while finishing this book and almost stopped writing it so I could write book 3! Kat will play a major role in the next book! No spoilers here. :)

I was going to call this book Fighting Magic because

they had to learn how to fight and use magic. I polled my newsletter subscribers and Hurricane of Magic was a huge winner! I hope you thought so as well.

Please consider leaving a review on Amazon or Goodreads for this book, or any book you read. Without reviews, authors don't know what you like or dislike about a book.

Sharing is caring! So be sure to tell your friends about The Voodoo Dolls!

www.ingramcontent.com/pod-product-compliance
Lightning Source LLC
Chambersburg PA
CBHW021959170626
46808CB00001B/224